What had gotten into him?

During the rodeo board meeting, thoughts of Erin kept creeping into Sawyer's head. When he passed the road leading to the Delong ranch, Sawyer decided to visit her. Besides, he could use the excuse that he wanted to ride. He was a cowboy.

He parked his truck and saw Erin in the corral, practicing her barrel racing. He sat and watched her ride the figure eights. Slipping out of his truck, he softly closed the door.

She didn't bounce in her saddle, nor did she yank on the reins. She leaned into the sharp turn, keeping her weight off the horse's back. They worked in unison as a well-oiled machine. When she finished the last figure eight, she let her horse canter around the corral, cooling both her and the horse.

"You've got a good seat," he said.

"Hours of practice."

Her face glowed and her entire body appeared relaxed and at ease, the most relaxed he'd ever seen her. This was a joyful woman, who loved riding and competing. As she came toward him, he felt himself being drawn to that smile.

Leann Harris has always had stories in her head. Once her youngest child went to school, she began putting those stories on a page. She is active in her local RWA chapter and ACFW chapters. She's a teacher of the deaf (high school), a master composter and avid gardener, and teaches writing at her local community college. Her website is leannharris.com.

Books by Leann Harris

Love Inspired

Rodeo Heroes

A Ranch to Call Home
A Rancher for Their Mom
The Cowboy Meets His Match

Second Chance Ranch
Redemption Ranch
Fresh-Start Ranch

Love Inspired Suspense

Hidden Deception
Guarded Secrets

Visit the Author Profile page at Harlequin.com for more titles.

The Cowboy Meets His Match

Leann Harris

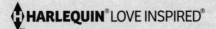

 LOVE INSPIRED BOOKS

Recycling programs
for this product may
not exist in your area.

ISBN-13: 978-0-373-81915-7

The Cowboy Meets His Match

Copyright © 2016 by Barbara M. Harrison

www.Harlequin.com

Printed in U.S.A.

Let the morning bring me word of
Your unfailing love, for I have put my trust in You.
—*Psalms* 143:8

For my grandbaby: You are the miracle child we prayed for, and your smile melts my heart.

Chapter One

Erin Joy Delong stood before the closed confer-
ence-room door. On the other side lay the truth
she needed to face no matter how ugly. Grasp-
ing the doorknob, she took a deep breath and
turned it.

All talking ceased. The air-conditioning
clicked on, filling the dead silence.

Erin looked at each of the seven men seated
around the table. No one would meet her gaze
except for the stranger standing at the head of
the table. A slide of his presentation on how to
reorganize the bicounty rodeo lit the screen behind him.

Her knees nearly buckled. She hadn't gotten
the job. No, the job of reorganizing the rodeo that
her great-grandfather established had gone to a
total stranger.

"Erin, we didn't expect you," Melvin Lowell,
the rodeo board's president, said.

She didn't doubt it. "Sorry I'm late, but after I talked with dad's doctors at the hospital this morning, I ran into a big accident on the interstate just outside Albuquerque. Then, finding this un-scheduled *Thursday* meeting proved tricky, since you'd moved it from the rodeo headquarters."

The men around the table shifted in their chairs as if they were ashamed of themselves. They continued to avoid her gaze.

"How's your father?" Mel asked, as if nothing was off-kilter.

She stepped into the elegant meeting room at the new conference center. "He's improving from the stroke, but we won't know the extent of the damage for several days. I drove in as his representative on the board."

"Is that legal?" Norman Burke, one of the board members from Harding County, asked. "I mean, if he can't talk—"

"You can call my mother or the floor nurse at the hospital, Sylvia Carter, who witnessed Dad nodding for me to represent him until he came back."

"Oh."

Erin glanced at the man giving the presentation and caught the hint of a smile that crossed his face before it disappeared.

The muted brush of her boots on the carpet was the only sound in the room as she walked to the empty chair on the opposite side of the table and sat. In front of her was a slick folder that read "*Tucumcari Rodeo Proposal* by Sawyer Jensen." Her eyes jerked up and clashed with Melvin's. He didn't look away.

"I take it Mr. Jensen won the contract?"

"Yes, we voted for him at the last meeting," Mel replied, his head held high. "Didn't anyone tell you?" Too much satisfaction laced his voice. Most of the other board members kept their gazes fixed on the table.

"No, but you know with all the chaos that occurred the day of the vote and Dad having the stroke afterward, it was the last thing on Mom's mind."

Norman Burke glared at Mel. "Cut it out, Lowell. The lady has more on her plate than this rodeo."

"Of course."

If Mel's words were meant to be accommodating, they failed.

"You don't have to stay, Erin, since we've already hired Sawyer. I'm sure you're tired after spending that much time at the hospital. But we wanted Sawyer to meet with us and show us his plan again and answer any further questions we had," Mel said.

Panic spread through the room. Several of the board members looked as if they wanted to escape, but retreat was the last thing on Erin's mind. Her hometown needed this revitalization. A successful rodeo would bring in much-needed people and revenue to help their bottom line.

"Thank you for your concern, Mel. But, as I said before, I'll be Dad's representative until he's well enough to come back."

A couple of men shifted in their chairs; throats were cleared, but no one said anything.

"Sawyer, why don't you continue explaining your overall plan to us?" Melvin said, ending the tense moment. "I'm sure Erin would like to hear it."

"We're on page three, Ms. Delong." Sawyer nodded to his presentation folder.

Fingering the folder, Erin studied Sawyer Jensen. The handsome man stood over six feet with sandy-brown hair and compelling hazel eyes that did funny things to her stomach, which she ignored. He had a scar on his chin below the corner of his mouth. When his eyes met hers, there was no smugness in those green depths, but admiration, instead. She didn't understand his reaction, but it eased the blow. As she studied the man, she had the feeling that she'd met him before.

Sawyer started to explain his strategy to save the rodeo and put it back in the black.

Chalking up her body's reaction to stress and the long drive this morning, Erin opened the folder. She tried to follow Sawyer's presentation, but it seemed she'd gone deaf and blind. Looking up through her lashes, she saw Melvin studying her. She would *not* cry in front of him or any of the other board members. Nor would she cry in front of this stranger. That wasn't Erin Delong's way. When her ex-boyfriend had announced, at their high school graduation, that he was engaged to Traci Lowell, Mel's daughter, she hadn't cried, much to Traci's disappointment. Maybe Traci's father thought he could make her cry this time. Of course, the meeting wasn't finished yet.

By the time they adjourned, Erin couldn't tell what Sawyer had said. For all she knew he could've suggested they burn the old rodeo grounds down and sell tickets to bring in money.

Most of the board members hurried to where Sawyer stood, taking a wide berth around her to shake Sawyer's hand and comment on his presentation. Their guilty faces made her wonder if they thought she'd throw a fit or break down in tears if they got too close. She could assure them that neither would happen, but they clearly weren't going to take any chances.

Only Chris Saddler stopped by where she stood.

"I'm sorry you didn't win, Erin. I voted for you to get the job. With you being local, and knowing the history of the rodeo and what resources we have, I thought you'd be best, instead of an outsider."

Chris was one of her dad's friends. She stood. "Thanks, Chris, and thanks for the heads-up this morning. Being at the hospital, you lose sense of time."

He opened his mouth to say something more, then closed it. He nodded and walked away.

Mel was the last one to shake Sawyer's hand. "A good presentation. If you have any questions, just call me, Sawyer."

Snatching the slick folder off the table, Erin headed for the door. Later, when she could think clearly, she'd read it over and evaluate his plan to see how it differed from hers.

"Ms. Delong?"

The deep voice calling her name sent shivers down her spine. It also stopped the other board members in their tracks at the door, no doubt expecting fireworks between her and Sawyer. Torn between wanting to plow through the bodies clogging the way out and facing the man with the wonderful rich voice, she straightened her shoulders, turned and faced him.

He stepped to her side. "Would you mind if we talked?"

Puzzled frowns crossed the board members' faces, and she heard a couple of them whisper.

"I'd love to, Mr. Jensen—"

"Sawyer is my first name."

"—Sawyer, but I last ate at seven this morning before visiting my dad in the hospital. After consulting with his doctors and my mother, I drove here. With the delay on the road, I never got the opportunity to eat. I'm probably not good company right now." Although it was only 1:40 p.m., food would help her thinking and dealing with this mess.

The man flashed a killer smile at her. "I haven't had anything, either, since breakfast in Amarillo, and I could use some sustenance, too. A full stomach helps me think and helps my attitude. Why don't we go and get a burger and talk?"

"So you think my attitude is bad?" she asked.

At the tone of her voice, groans erupted from the men at the door.

"No," Sawyer answered evenly. "I was talking about myself. And when I'm hungry, I don't listen well."

More groans.

She nodded. "Understandable."

His eyes twinkled.

Erin didn't know whether to grin at his cheekiness or ignore him. "What's there to talk about? You won."

"Well, with your late arrival, you didn't get to hear my complete proposal and I wanted the opportunity to discuss some of my ideas with you. Since you put in a bid, I'd like to get your reaction."

Was he teasing her? Did he want to rub her nose in her failure? She searched his face for any sign of duplicity, but found nothing. She needed some time to process all this, but she wouldn't let the board members see her disappointment. "I'm going next door to Lulu's Burgers. If you want to join me, I won't object."

The man didn't take offense at her tone. "Give me a second to unplug my computer and projector and pack them up."

So the equipment was his. She'd wondered where the board had found money to buy such nice equipment. "I'll be waiting next door."

She walked through the crowd of gawking faces clustered at the door, Mel's being the most outraged. Too bad.

Well, he'd been in more awkward places than this, Sawyer thought, but not many. There'd been that time, in Nevada, when the man who'd hired him to turn around the Western Days Rodeo had his wife and sister barge into the meeting and start screaming at each other. The women hadn't stopped screeching long enough for him to understand what the fight was about. Things quickly went physical, and the women threw anything they could get their hands on. Sawyer ducked a cowboy statue, but the owner wasn't as lucky and was coldcocked by a glass paperweight thrown by his wife. Of course, as a turnaround specialist, Sawyer had been in his fair share of tense situations and been able to bring the warring sides together.

Sawyer had seen the shock and sadness flash in

Erin's eyes before the protective shield came up to cover her emotions. His heart went out to her, or maybe it was just plain attraction that struck him like a fist to the chin. After his brother's recent marriage, Sawyer realized how alone he was now, and a restlessness settled inside him. The brothers hadn't really had a home since that little apartment behind the church in Plainview in the Texas Panhandle, but it hadn't mattered because they'd been a team. Together against the world. But now?

"You're not going to have lunch with that woman, are you?" Melvin walked back into the room.

Sawyer grabbed his laptop and the projector. "I am."

"Why?"

"Because I'm hungry."

Melvin sputtered. "But you won."

Sawyer nodded toward the outside glass door. Melvin opened it. When Sawyer had arrived this morning, he'd driven to the rodeo board's office, then followed Melvin to the new convention facility.

"Winning makes a poor lunch, Mel, and when Erin mentioned food, my hunger hit me like a kick from the old mule my dad worked with. And since the place is right here, why not eat?"

Melvin opened his mouth, but nothing came out.

"Besides, I'd think you'd want me to see if I

could win the woman over, get her on my side. It will make things operate smoothly. I don't want any disruptions."

"Well, yes, but—"

"I'm glad you agree. It will make things better later on."

Sawyer stored his equipment in the long steel toolbox that ran the width of the bed of his truck. Turning, he faced Melvin and waited for the rest of his comment.

"Well?"

Mel glared. "Don't be surprised if she bites your ear off and spits it out."

"I'll consider myself warned."

Mel gave a curt nod and strolled to his car.

Sawyer's curiosity about Erin was piqued as he walked to the restaurant. His competition for this job was certainly much better looking than the one for the last job. Of course, from all the panicked looks thrown at Erin when she'd walked into the room, and from the dire warning just issued, he'd have to be on guard. The lady wasn't just a pretty face. But, as he thought about it, Sawyer couldn't shake the feeling that he'd met Erin somewhere before. Where, he couldn't say, but—

When he opened the door to Lulu's, the smell of burgers smacked him in the face, making his mouth water. Chrome-and-Formica tables à la 1950s vintage dotted the restaurant, with several booths by the windows. A jukebox sat close to the front door. Pictures from previous rodeos hung on the walls, along with ribbons from different 4-H projects. In the center of one wall was a large picture of Erin racing around a barrel, her long hair flying from beneath her cowgirl hat, her elbows out and her body low over the neck of the horse. A ribbon hung off the corner of the picture with a plaque below announcing State Champion. The picture impressed him. The lady knew her way around a rodeo, that was for sure, and he knew she'd have some ideas.

In a booth by the windows sat Erin. As he approached the table, she pointed to the opposite wall. "If you want to eat, you have to order at the counter behind you."

She wasn't going to make this easy, but, oddly enough, that didn't put a damper on his spirit.

He glanced over his shoulder. A large menu covered the wall behind the order counter. He turned back to her. "Recommend anything?"

"Try Lulu's chili burger."

He nodded and ordered the burger. When he joined her, he noticed that she had opened his proposal. Sliding onto the bench across from her, he asked, "What do you think?"

"That you know how to put together a proposal."

"That's it?"

She placed her forearms on the tabletop and

leaned forward. "I haven't read it all. Your slick marketing diverted my attention."

He didn't think she meant it as a compliment, but he couldn't help smiling. He'd impressed her. "Well, it's geared to do that."

"Let's see if the sleek outside matches what's inside." She looked down at the presentation.

If he didn't miss his guess, it would take a lot to win over this woman. He didn't mind competing with others for a job, but he would've liked to have known there was a hometown applicant in the running against him.

He studied her while she read his plan. The lady's long dark hair hung as a single thick braid down her back. If he didn't miss his guess, she had Native American blood flowing through her veins, but with a name like Delong, he wondered. She must be five foot seven or eight, since she stood just at the right height for him to kiss her with ease. The thought startled him and he must've made some sound.

"What?" she demanded.

He waved away the question. "Nothing."

She went back to reading.

Kissing her? That crazy thought had to be fallout from the wild morning he'd had, combined with his brother's recent marriage. Caleb's main focus now would be his wife, and the new baby they were expecting. But it left Sawyer feeling at loose ends. The brothers had depended on each other to survive their teen years. Well, they weren't teenagers anymore, but Sawyer felt a certain part of himself missing.

"I know you haven't had time to completely look over my proposal," he blurted out, "but did you have any follow-up questions to the presentation I made? Is there anything you might not have been comfortable asking in the presence of the others that I can answer now?"

The instant the last word fell out of his mouth, he knew he'd stepped in it. The fire in her eyes blazed. "I didn't mean—"

"Understand, Mr. Jensen, I don't suffer from shyness. I know my mind and will speak it. But I don't go off half-cocked, either. I'll know what I'm talking about when I open my mouth." She leaned in. "There's an old saying about keeping your powder dry until ready to fire. That's me."

He wanted to smile but resisted the urge. He knew better than to throw gas on a fire, but her strong spirit attracted him like metal filings to a magnet. "Good to know."

He had to admire her reaction. She didn't go ballistic, cry or stomp out of the meeting room like his last girlfriend would've or his mother. It looked as if she would give him a fair hearing. The thought surprised him. He sat back. Glancing over at the wall, he saw her picture again. "When did you win your ribbon?" he said, diverting his thoughts.

She glanced up. He nodded to her picture.

"Oh, that ribbon—high school."

Meaning she'd won a lot more. "Lulu helped sponsor me that year at the state fair. Since she helped, and raised money for me, I thought she should get the ribbon."

"I understand. My winnings helped put me through college. I competed in the summer and between semesters to earn enough money for school."

"Really?"

"I do know my way around a lasso."

With a thawing of her coolness, she leaned forward.

He thought he caught a hint of respect. "I'm not just some college-educated busybody who thinks he knows how to solve the world's problems. My brother and I have been rodeoing since we were both teens." He rested his hand on the table. "I've lived it. The last time I worked and competed was last June in the little town of Peaster, Texas."

Her eyes widened in an 'aha' moment. "You were at the charity rodeo?"

"I was. I worked in tandem with my brother, riding pickup."

"I was there, too, competing in barrel racing. Talked with the organizer, Brenda Kaye, about how she put together the rodeo, hoping to pick up some ideas on how to save our rodeo."

"Brenda did a great job. When my brother confessed he wanted to marry her, I cheered."

"She's your sister-in-law?"

"She is, and getting her degree in counseling. She's an Iraqi war veteran and wants to help fellow vets."

Erin's expression softened, making him feel less like the monster who'd stomped her dreams.

The waitress showed up with a burger. "Here you go, Erin." The teenage girl placed the plate on the table. "Yours will be out in a minute, sir."

"If my burger is as good as this one smells, I can't wait." He grinned at her. "And my name's Sawyer. *Sir* makes me feel old."

She nodded. "I'm Rose. Mom cooks the best burgers in this part of New Mexico. Really, she's the best cook hands down." A ding of "order up" sounded and the girl disappeared.

Erin grabbed a French fry and popped it into her mouth as she continued to study his proposal.

The waitress appeared again with his burger. "Here you go, Sawyer. Enjoy."

"Are you still doing the work/study program in high school?" Erin asked Rose.

"Yup, and I have a ton of ideas I want Mom to try." She walked back to the kitchen with a little spring in her step.

Erin bowed her head, silently asking a blessing.

Sawyer liked that and joined her. When he looked up, she studied him.

He didn't say anything, but picked up the hamburger and took a bite. The flavors of chili and meat danced on his tongue. "You weren't kidding."

"Sawyer, I'm known for a lot of things, but being funny isn't one of them."

"So you don't laugh?" He took another bite of his burger. He felt some chili slide down his chin.

"How's the burger?" A rawboned woman stood at the end of the table. From her posture, the woman knew her way around the restaurant and wasn't afraid of hard work. She smiled when she saw the chili on his chin. "Ah, I see you're enjoying my special burger."

Wiping his chin, he nodded to Erin. "She wasn't fooling when she said this burger is the best."

The woman blushed. "Thank you. Our Erin is a treasure. Anyone who has a problem talks to her for ideas and advice."

"You're going to be seeing a lot of me in the next few weeks," he said after swallowing.

"Erin, did you acquire a new boyfriend that you didn't tell us about?"

Erin choked on her tea.

"No. He's not mine," she shot back. "Ask Mel about him."

Lulu frowned. "You're not making any sense."

Sawyer grabbed another napkin from the dispenser, wiped his hand and chin, then held out his hand to the woman. "I'm Sawyer Jensen. I've been hired to work on your rodeo."

"You didn't win the job?" Lulu glanced at Erin. "You okay with that?"

Erin sat quietly and studied Sawyer. "I'll let you know after I've read his proposal."

Eyes narrowed, Lulu focused on him. "You've got some mighty big shoes to fill, mister. Like I said, folks around here tend to depend on Erin."

Sawyer now knew that he wasn't the odds-on favorite of some of the people in town. He'd have to turn on the charm. "I'll try, ma'am. And I hope to consult with Erin here after she has finished reading my proposal."

"I'd like to hear her ideas, myself. Not that I don't trust you, but we know Erin."

"No offense taken."

"How is your father?" Lulu asked.

"The doctors think he'll recover, but how quickly they don't know. Right now they are still evaluating him. He's conscious, but not talking."

Lulu nodded. "I'm sorry about that. If you need anything, let me know."

Erin let down her guard long enough that he saw the worry in her eyes. "Thanks."

He took another bite of the burger, which confirmed what his taste buds had already told him. "Oh, this is good."

Several more locals entered the restaurant and clustered at the order desk.

Erin nodded at them.

Sawyer wanted to ask her about a good place to stay, but he wasn't sure she'd welcome giving him more advice.

Taking the last bite of her burger, she threw her napkin on her plate. "I'll finish your proposal tonight and get back to you after I've thought about your suggestions and plan of attack."

A reasonable response, but he'd keep up his guard. "Do you still ride barrels competitively?"

"I do and was in Denver competing when I got word about my dad's stroke." She fell silent. "Five days," she whispered to herself. She shook her head and picked up her thoughts. "I left the competition and dropped my horse at our family ranch before driving to see Dad. I didn't know the result of the vote on the contract until this morning when I saw you standing at the head of the table."

He tensed.

"Congratulations." She held out her hand.

He took it, and he felt an electric charge race up his arm, scrambling his brains. "Thank you. I welcome all input."

"Really?" Her arched brow and the twinkle in her eyes gave him pause. He knew a challenge when he saw one.

"Absolutely. Once you've read through my plan, I'd welcome your input."

"If you're pulling my leg or trying to smooth

things over with the little lady, you've seriously misjudged the situation."

"No, I meant what I said."

"Good, because I'll have input."

"I look forward to it."

Her mouth slowly curved into a smile that could only be categorized as one of pure determination.

The door to the restaurant opened and a couple around Erin's age walked in. The woman had beautiful blond hair that fell beyond her shoulders. Under the ton of makeup she had slathered on, she might've been pretty, Sawyer thought, but she just looked hard. She scanned the restaurant, clapped eyes on them and marched to the table much like General Patton marching across France.

"Erin, what a wonderful heart you have." The woman's voice dripped with sugar and venom. "I could've never eaten with the man who beat me out for a job I wanted, but here you are dining with our new turnaround specialist," she said. Her raised voice echoed through the restaurant. The smirk on her face told Sawyer this woman enjoyed Erin's humiliation.

Erin didn't look up as she calmly collected the proposal and put it into her tote. The man with the blonde looked panicked.

Sawyer held out his hand. "Sawyer Jensen. And you are?"

"Traci and Andy Hyatt," the man responded.

"My father is Melvin Lowell," Traci announced, as if that said it all.

Sawyer stole a look at Erin. She didn't look nervous or upset. She simply sat back.

Andy cleared his throat. "I'm sorry to hear about your dad, Erin. I always liked him."

Traci elbowed her husband.

"What?" Andy asked. "Detrick always treated me well. I'm sorry to hear about his stroke."

"Thanks, Andy," Erin replied. "Dad felt the same about you."

There was a wealth of meaning buried in those words. Andy glanced at his wife, who glared back.

"Watch your back with this one. You might find a knife there," Traci warned, pointing toward Erin.

Andy pulled his wife away from the table. "Let's order."

Erin didn't offer any explanation, but the tension the couple caused lingered.

In a small town there were lots of undercurrents that could take down an outsider in an instant, and Sawyer had just encountered one. You had to pay attention to body language and tone if you wanted to save yourself. He'd learned that lesson the hard way with his mom's constant stream of boyfriends.

"Can you recommend a place to stay while I'm here?" he asked, wanting to change the subject.

Erin's gaze settled back on him. "The board didn't arrange a place for you to stay?"

"No, it wasn't mentioned."

"Well, there are quite a few motels."

"What about that interesting-looking motel I saw a block over when I drove into town? The one that looks like a big sombrero?"

"Are you sure you want to stay there? It was built in 1937. We have more modern places."

"No, I kinda like its style. A blast from the past."

"Most of the rooms don't have TVs. And their phones are the big black rotary kind."

For some reason, the lady didn't want him to stay there. Why?

Before he could respond, a couple walked into the restaurant. They nodded to Erin and made their way to the order counter.

"I think I can handle that," he said.

Erin studied him, but before she could respond, they heard, "What?" The man at the counter said, "You're joshing me?" He looked over his shoulder at them.

"You sure, Lulu?" the woman questioned.

Instantly, the couple walked over to their table.

"You didn't win, Erin?" the man asked. "This is the stranger who won?" They looked from Erin to Sawyer.

Sawyer felt the gazes of the couple boring into his back.

"I can't believe the board voted for a stranger over one of our own, especially after what happened with your father," the woman added.

"It was a fair vote," Traci called out from across the room.

The man glared at her. "I think we all know how you feel."

Sawyer heard a strangled protest.

The man ignored it and focused on him and Erin. "Why go with a stranger? I know you and trust that your ideas would save the rodeo."

"I've just skimmed his plan, Bob, but I wouldn't jump to a conclusion before I've really studied it and thought about what he plans to do."

Bob considered Erin's suggestion. "Sounds good to me. I think the board needs to have a meeting tonight to let the rest of the town listen to this man's ideas. The longer we don't know what he wants to do, the longer we'll be in the dark, and I want to know what's happening from the beginning." He whipped out his cell phone and punched in a number.

Erin sat quietly as they listened to Bob.

"Mel, I just learned that you gave the contract for the rodeo to a stranger." He paused, obviously listening to Mel. "Okay, Sawyer Jensen."

Everyone in the restaurant listened, but Sawyer watched Erin's expression. Her defense of him to Bob surprised him. She wanted to give him a chance. He didn't know what to think or feel.

Bob nodded. "I think that's an excellent idea. I'll call around and we'll get enough people together tonight to listen to this man's ideas. At seven."

Another look passed between Erin and Sawyer.

"That's no excuse. If the board members from Harding want the same for their residents, they can do it tomorrow." Silence. "You may be head of the board, but that can be revoted."

Traci's gasp sounded through the room.

"Good. We'll gather tonight at the new conference center." Bob hung up and nailed Sawyer with a look. "We're going to listen to you tonight. You got a problem with that?"

"No, I'd welcome the opportunity to present my proposal to the residents."

"Good." Bob glanced at Erin. "I couldn't do less than check this guy out."

"Thanks, Bob."

"You always favored her, Bob," Traci shouted.

"And if you'd driven my son around while I was in the hospital and my wife was with me, then I might've favored you, too, Traci."

No comment came from the table behind them.

"Come on, honey. I'm hungry," his wife said.

With a final look, the couple walked back to the order window.

Sawyer knew it was time to leave. "I'd like to check into that motel."

"You sure?" Erin said.

"I am."

Shrugging, she stood and walked outside. "We could walk, but you probably have luggage and equipment that you need to put in your room, so we'll drive."

He nodded. "I'd like to ask one question."

Her shoulders tensed.

"Who's Bob?"

She visibly relaxed. "Robert Rivera owns the hardware/feed/tractor store. If you need something for your ranch or farm, chances are Bob has it or can order it or knows where to get it."

"And he's not on the rodeo board?"

"He used to be, but family stuff has kept him busy, so he resigned. He was on the board with my father and they usually voted against Mel. It made things lively."

"I'm sure it did."

"And be warned, things could get vocal tonight."

"I'll consider myself warned."

He swallowed his smile. She may have thought she could scare him away, but she didn't know who he was. His professional reputation as a man who could bring success out of defeat and turmoil was at stake. But more than that, there was something here in this town that called to him and he wasn't going to ignore that call. He'd turn the rodeo around and make it thrive. And the beautiful woman who would challenge him had nothing to do with it, he reassured himself.

It took less than three minutes for them to drive over to the next block and park in front of The Sombrero Motel, a prime example of art deco. The lobby was shaped like the high conical crown of a sombrero, surrounded by the curved brim of the hat sporting red, green and yellow stripes at its base. The hotel's color resembled a big swimming pool.

Erin still couldn't believe he wanted to stay here instead of one of the newer places. "Change your mind?"

"Nope. This place looks great." He carefully ran his gaze over the building.

"Carmen Vega, the owner, bought it ten years ago, when she came back from Denver after working for several different hotel chains. She grew up seeing The Sombrero and had always loved it, so she bought it and restored it."

"Good to know."

Pushing open the glass door, Erin called out, "Hey, Lencho, how's it going?"

The young college-aged man looked up from

his reading. "Erin, what are you doing here?" He stood.

"I've brought you a paying customer."

"Good, things are kinda slow right now, but next week, we've got more people coming in. The historic-motel crowd of Southern California has booked the place."

Erin made the introductions, and Lencho handed Sawyer an old-fashioned registration card used circa 1937.

Sawyer stared down at it.

"Carmen believes in the full-blown experience," Erin explained.

Sawyer shrugged and went to work filling out the card.

Erin leaned over the counter. "What are you studying, Lencho?"

"Differential equations. I have to have it for the engineering degree."

Erin laughed. "I had a couple of courses that I could've done without in college. But fortunately I grabbed one of the bowling slots as my PE."

It took Sawyer less than two minutes to fill out the card.

Erin peeked at it. "No TV?"

"I want the full experience." If she thought she'd scared him, apparently she was wrong.

Lencho pulled the key out of a cubbyhole behind the registration desk. "You want me to show you to the room?"

Erin laughed. "If he can't find room two, the board's going to be in real trouble and needs to rethink giving him the rodeo job."

The youth stilled. "He got the job? I thought you applied for it."

She shrugged.

"But we're having an impromptu meeting tonight for the town folks to review my plan," Sawyer explained. "Please come."

"Bob organized it," Erin added.

The youth looked from Sawyer to her. "I'll be there. I don't want to miss any of that action." He rubbed his hands together. "We haven't had so much excitement since Denise Sander's burro got loose, ended up in Melvin's yard and ate the flowers, tomatoes and chilies growing in his garden."

Lencho gave Sawyer the key, an actual old-fashioned metal key.

"I haven't seen anything like this in a long time."

Erin's brow arched. "Full experience, remember?"

"True."

Motioning Sawyer outside, they walked the seventeen steps to room two. The motel consisted of twelve rooms with the sombrero-shaped lobby anchoring the east end of the structure.

The twelve rooms surrounded a central patio covered by a pergola and scattered with various cacti. Massive Mexican clay pots dotted the patio area along with concrete benches decorated with Mexican tile. Room twelve anchored the far end of the three-sided structure. The lobby stood closest to the old Route 66.

"I'm impressed." He motioned to the patio.

"Carmen and her uncle landscaped the courtyard after they finished the rooms, using original plans the owners had drawn up when the motel was built."

They stopped at the door of room two, and he unlocked it. Stepping inside, he slowly surveyed the cool interior. The slick lines of the desk and chairs could've come from any of the *Thin Man* movies popular in the thirties. No TV, and a big black phone on the desk. Beside it was a Tiffany-style lamp with a cut-glass shade of brown, yellow and orange glass. A wonderful painting of the desert landscape at sundown hung on the wall over the bed. She loved this decor, but he didn't say anything.

"Does this meet with your approval?" She grinned at him, enjoying his reaction or nonreaction. She'd warned him.

He didn't bat an eye. "This is fine. Is there a Wi-Fi connection somewhere close?"

"In the lobby."

"Thanks for the heads-up."

"I hope you keep that positive attitude when we meet later tonight."

"I'm looking forward to it." No hesitation colored his response.

She wanted to grin. "I hope so."

Chapter Two

Erin had finally managed to find her footing. Her father's stroke had tilted her world off its axis, but when she had raced to the board headquarters today and found nobody there, she'd known another blow was around the corner. Talking to Mel's secretary about where they were, Erin knew. She thought she'd been prepared for the blow of losing out on the job she so wanted, but the instant she opened the door and saw Sawyer standing at the head of the table, she realized she wasn't. Why hadn't her dad called her with the news? How soon after the meeting had the stroke happened? Mother wasn't clear on the details.

She shook off the trivial thoughts. What was important was that her father had survived the stroke, not that she hadn't gotten the job. They'd spent countless hours on the phone, talking about what needed to be done in the update. He'd mentioned the other candidate that Melvin brought in, but Dad thought it wouldn't be a problem, at least the last time they talked, which was a few days before the vote.

She'd tap-danced her way through today's board meeting.

Pushing open the lobby door, she looked at Lencho. "How are you doing in your classes? Are you keeping up your grades?" Her dad had tutored the young man his freshman year in high school.

"I'm okay." He looked through the glass door and watched as Sawyer moved his truck from the far side of the office to park in front of his room. "How do you feel about that guy?"

She shrugged. "I'll be interested in hearing his plans tonight."

"I'm sorry that you didn't get the job."

Erin realized that the young man felt uncomfortable that she didn't win. "Don't worry. I'm not surrendering. I'll keep him on track. You remember, we didn't let you flunk out of algebra. Well, I'm not simply going to walk away from the rodeo and give up."

"No matter how much Traci lobbied for the other guy?"

The kid wasn't telling Erin anything she hadn't already figured out. "You got it."

"Good. Of course, I was surprised the guy didn't take the room with the TV."

"I guess we have a lot to learn about him."

"True."

"Does he know anything about rodeo?" Lencho asked.

Mel wasn't going to foist any greenhorn on the community, not even to please his daughter. "He does. He claims to have won several events at different rodeos."

The kid brightened. "Let's look him up on the internet." He opened his laptop and did a search on Sawyer's name. Erin walked around the counter and peered over his shoulder. Sawyer's name came up in the search engine along with a listing of his wins.

They silently read the list. He'd made a name for himself.

"Well, you're right. He's no greenhorn." Pointing to the computer screen, Lencho said, "He's got a brother, too, who did pickup."

"He told me."

They read about Sawyer's brother.

Taking a deep breath, Lencho shook his head. "He looks like the real deal."

He did, indeed, and from what they'd learned about Sawyer's and his brother's backgrounds, they were the real deal who participated in rodeo. Sawyer had the credentials to know what the cowboys needed, but Erin knew *this* rodeo and *these* people and knew the background that Sawyer didn't. "We'll find out tonight."

* * *

Erin tried to listen to the car radio on her drive home and ignore what had happened at the board meeting. She started to hum with Tim McGraw about heading down this road again.

But her wounded heart refused to let go of the hurt.

What had been the final tally of the board members? She knew Melvin hadn't voted for her. Of course, his daughter thought Erin was a cross between Godzilla and Cinderella's stepmother, but that stemmed from Traci's unreasonable fear that Erin would steal back Traci's husband, since he'd been Erin's high school sweetheart. Andy had wanted to marry Erin, but she hadn't wanted to settle down so soon. Going to college had been her goal but, no matter what she said to Andy, he never took her seriously. Traci often told Erin what a good catch Andy was and why not marry him? Traci thought Erin had lost her marbles not to take up Andy's offer. The instant he broke up with Erin, Traci swept in and captured her man. Erin had not been invited to the wedding even though it had been a Christmas affair. When Erin returned home the first time after she started college, Traci made it clear their friendship was over, much to Erin's surprise. Why Traci acted the way she did, Erin didn't understand. She got her man and Erin got to go to college.

How many other members of the board had followed Mel's lead in voting for Sawyer? Why had they voted for an outsider instead of a hometown girl? That's what hurt the most.

It's business, the logical part of her brain argued, but her heart said the vote was against her personally, not her proposal.

Pulling off the main road, she drove down the drive to the ranch house and parked her truck under the covered carport and breezeway that ran from the kitchen to the barn.

She didn't go into the house, and instead walked to the corral behind the barn to see her horse, Wind Dancer. The moment the horse saw Erin, she trotted over to the fence and head butted her.

Reaching out, Erin stroked the horse's neck. "Did you miss me, girl? I'm sure Santo took care of you." The horse arched her neck and then raced around the ring, coming to a stop in front of her.

Looking down at her long skirt and boots, she realized she needed to change. "Give me a minute, Dancer, and I'll be back."

It took less than five minutes for her to grab her bag from the truck, change into jeans and race back outside. Her brother, Tate, hadn't come home from school yet, and Erin didn't know where her aunt Betty was, but they'd show up.

Erin didn't bother with a saddle. She grabbed reins and a halter, opened the gate and slipped them on Dancer. Erin hopped on Dancer and rode out of the corral. Horse and rider started slowly, and then Erin leaned close to the horse's neck as Dancer picked up speed. They were in their element, racing across the high desert, dancing on the wind.

Erin could feel herself touch the face of heaven, giving up her wound and the hurt of not winning the contract to reorganize the rodeo.

Finally, Dancer slowed to a walk and stopped. Leaning over, Erin rested her head on the horse's neck. "I was blindsided when I walked into that meeting, girl. Felt as naked as the day I was born." She sat up. "So what am I going to do now?" She looked to heaven. "I need some direction here, Lord. I don't know what to do, but I know I'm not giving up." She thought for a moment and remembered the look of admiration in Sawyer's eyes when she'd initially faced off with Mel. There was something about the man that intrigued her and drew her. It didn't make sense, but then nothing in the past few days did. It was one of those times when you just held on to God and knew He'd guide you through the storm.

"Of course, Bob did set up the meeting tonight, so I need some wisdom there."

The instant the words were out of her mouth, she knew what she needed to do and that wasn't feeling sorry for herself.

Sawyer finished storing his things in the room and remembered how Erin had watched him as he'd registered at the historic motel and surveyed his room. If he didn't miss his guess, she'd thought he'd call uncle and go to one of the newer chains. As he'd played along and taken the room, he'd discovered that he liked it. She intrigued him. He didn't know what he'd expected when she'd appeared in the conference room, but it wasn't the woman he encountered. He didn't know quite what to make of her, but he had a feeling he'd find out. He'd walk cautiously around her until he knew what to expect. Would she be fair—or fight dirty like his mom and last girlfriend? He'd had enough of clingy and manipulative women.

Walking back to the lobby, Sawyer found Lencho hadn't moved from the desk and his homework.

"Is the room okay?"

Oddly enough, the room had the feeling of home—strong, sturdy, something that would be there for a long time. He hadn't had that experience growing up until his big brother had taken responsibility for the two of them. "It's great."

The kid studied him as if he didn't believe his ears.

"What I need are directions to the rodeo fairgrounds."

Lencho pointed to the brochure stand in the corner of the room. "You'll find maps there."

Sawyer retrieved a brochure and laid it out on the counter.

"So you beat out Erin for the rodeo job?"

Sawyer looked up and studied the youth. "I did."

"I'm surprised. I mean, everyone in town knows if you need something done, Erin's the one who can do it. And she always comes through."

"So I hear." He had his work cut out for him to win people over. "But maybe the board wanted someone who isn't familiar with anything here to look at the situation with new eyes. Suppose you're looking at one of your equations and can't see how to solve it. You've worked and worked on how to get the answer, then someone else looks at it and sees where you've gone wrong and points it out. The same is true with the rodeo. Maybe someone who's not familiar with it can see a problem, or even just do it a different way, and solve the situation."

Lencho thought about it. "That makes sense."

Sawyer studied the map to orient himself with the streets.

Pointing to where they were, Lencho said, "Go down to First Street, turn right, and when you get to US 66, turn west and on the outskirts of town you should find the fairgrounds."

"Thanks."

He followed Lencho's directions and, within ten minutes, found the grounds. On the north side sat the rodeo arena with chutes and corrals, and on the south side stood the football field. In between the two sat a midway with accompanying food stands and game booths.

After parking his truck, he walked through the grounds, inspecting the facility. It wasn't in bad shape but needed upgrades. He pulled out his cell phone and took pictures to document the conditions. As he stood on the bleachers, he could imagine Erin on her horse, flying around the barrels in the main arena. He would have liked to see that.

The thought caught him off guard. He was the last person on earth she'd want to run into, he imagined, unless it was an opportunity to offer her suggestions. Still, he would've loved to watch her race. Maybe he could in the future.

He sat and pulled a small notebook out of his shirt pocket and jotted some notes. Later, when he was back in his room, he'd update his Power-Point, giving his initial thoughts, and incorporate the pictures he took this afternoon, pointing out how he'd redo the midway and food stands. He put the phone in his shirt pocket and headed back to his truck. He wanted to assess the roads leading into the rodeo grounds, which needed to be included in his overall plan, but as he drove away, he kept thinking of seeing Erin ride. When he worked on a rodeo, he never let his personal feelings interfere. There were a couple of times when the ladies he'd worked with wanted to take the relationship to another level, but he never did.

But this time—he stopped the thought cold.

What was wrong with him? Since his brother's wedding, Sawyer had been having all sorts of weird thoughts, and he chalked up his reaction to Erin as post-wedding blues. Did men get those? Surely that was the explanation.

Stepping into the house after her ride, Erin ran into Aunt Betty. Her salt-and-pepper hair hung in two braids, tied off with twine. Her colorful skirt and white blouse, belted at the waist, were her normal garb. Auntie preferred traditional Navajo dress. Besides, she teased, she couldn't fit into jeans the way Erin and her sister, Kai, could.

Mother had called her sister after Dad's stroke to come and watch over Erin's younger brother, Tate, a senior in high school. Mom thought Tate needed Betty's calming influence. Erin knew she should've come back with Auntie and Tate on Sunday, but wanted to stay to see how her father responded to the treatment the hospital provided.

"There you are. When I didn't find you, I knew you were out on Dancer."

"I can't fool you, can I?" Brushing a kiss across her aunt's cheek, Erin walked to the sink and got a large glass of water.

Betty studied her. "What's wrong, Daughter?"

In her mother's family, grown aunts and cousins called the younger members of the family *Daughter* or *Son*. It meant you were never alone and always had eyes on you, which was both a blessing and a pain. Erin thought about trying to divert her aunt's question, but no one got anything by Aunt Betty or Mother. They were nabbed every time they tried. Erin and her sister had learned not to try. Unfortunately, their brother, Tate, hadn't.

"I went to the board meeting in Dad's place. They hired the other person who applied for the job."

"What's the matter with those men?" Betty shook her head. "Someone should knock them in the head. They know you and how you've given to this town. If someone wants something done, you get a call, and that includes the children of board members. And they are not shy about asking for your help. You remember when Mel asked you to help Traci get through Algebra One? He wanted her to pass the class, but with you and your father tutoring her, she made a B minus. And then there was Chris Saddler's boy wanting help with his science project—"

"That's enough, Auntie. It's done." Erin didn't want to dwell on what was. She slipped her arms around her shorter, rounder aunt. "Thanks for believing in me," Erin whispered into her aunt's hair.

"You carry too much on those small shoulders. Not every problem is yours to solve, Daughter."

Erin stepped back, blinking her eyes. "True, but I have ideas on how to help the rodeo, and I cannot turn away. Besides, Dad wanted me to take his place on the board."

Shaking her finger, Betty said, "Rest and take care of yourself. We don't need another bird with a broken wing. With your father in the hospital, your mother needs you whole."

Erin couldn't deny that, but so far, her mom appeared to be bearing up under the load. "How is Tate doing?"

Betty didn't answer. She walked to the table and sat down. Erin joined her.

"What's wrong?" Her brother's freshman year in high school had been rough, and he'd given her parents no end of trouble, with skipping school and not wanting to go to church with them. But he wasn't given a choice whether or not to go to school and church. So he'd gone, and his sophomore and junior years had been better. He'd been doing well until their dad's stroke, then retreated into himself.

"Your brother acts as if nothing happened and life is fine. But I see behind the mask he's wearing. There's much trouble in his heart."

"I've worried about that. Kai mentioned he acted as if he didn't have a care in the world while at the hospital before I got there. She said he'd even disappeared for a couple of hours and no one could find him." Erin shook her head. "We all know he's hurting, Auntie, but—"

"I thought he seemed off when I picked him up at the hospital Sunday night, but he said nothing to me on the ride home," Betty said, shaking her head.

"He's a man—a young one," Erin defended, "but a man. When was the last time your husband sat down and talked to you when he was troubled about something?"

Betty smiled. "You're right."

"The town's having an impromptu meeting tonight about the rodeo. I'd like to shower and change clothes before going back."

Betty narrowed her eyes, making Erin feel guilty. "What's the name of this person who won the rodeo contract over you?"

"Sawyer Jensen."

"I think I should go to this meeting, too, even though I don't live here. Your mother might want my observations."

"You sure you want to go?"

Betty's eyes twinkled. "There's more going on than rodeo discussion."

True, there were lots of undercurrents, but if Erin didn't attend it might look like she was hiding—and that wasn't happening. Besides, Sawyer might need her to referee. The thought made her grin. She discounted her reaction to the man.

"You're right, but I'm afraid the meeting will not be a peaceful one."

Betty shooed the concern away. "Have I ever been known to run from a challenge?"

"No, Auntie." And that's what made Erin nervous.

It appeared the entire town of Tucumcari had turned out for the impromptu meeting that night. Sawyer had his presentation cued up on his computer and plugged into the overhead projector. He'd added a couple of slides he'd taken this afternoon to bolster his points on the changes he thought needed to be made.

A wave of sound ran through the audience. Sawyer glanced up and saw Erin, an older woman and a teenage boy walk into the room. People pointed the group to the front row, where several seats were left empty. The trio made their way forward.

The older woman stopped at the edge of the stage and waved Sawyer forward. Erin stood behind the woman, but the youth walked over to the empty seat and threw himself down. He shot Sawyer a look that said he was bored. His body language echoed his disdain at having to be there.

Sawyer moved to the edge of the stage, then jumped down. "Ma'am. I'm Sawyer Jensen. And you are?"

"Betty Crow Creek."

He glanced over at Erin.

Betty cleared her throat. "I'm Erin's aunt. I'm here while Erin's mother is in Albuquerque with her husband."

Sawyer held out his hand. "It's nice to meet you."

Betty shook it. "You appear normal. Really, a handsome man."

Erin blinked.

To cover his surprise, Sawyer smiled. "Thank you."

Betty folded her arms over her chest. "I expected someone who had two heads and was maybe green."

Sawyer's eyes widened.

"Auntie!" Erin's strangled protest could be heard only by Betty and him.

His mouth twitched with humor. "Am I the ogre you were led to believe?"

"Erin only said you won. In *my* mind I expected a monster who'd turned my niece's world upside down." Betty glanced at Erin, and then turned back to him. "I'm the one who imagined you with green skin and living under a bridge."

So far, he was batting zero.

Melvin stood, stepped to the podium and started the meeting. Betty and Erin took their seats. Showtime.

* * *

Twenty minutes later, after Sawyer finished his program, he opened for questions.

Erin had listened carefully to the plan Sawyer laid out. She had to admit he'd thought of some aspects of the rodeo that she hadn't and his plans were good.

Bob stood. "Have you actually been to the fairgrounds yourself?"

"I went this afternoon and updated the slides in the presentation," Sawyer answered. "The board sent pictures so I could evaluate the situation, but after seeing it myself I changed and tailored some of my ideas for this facility."

"I can vouch for that," Melvin added.

Bob didn't look convinced.

A brisk discussion followed, with people asking questions and commenting on the presentation.

Bob stood again. "I'd like to hear Erin's plan, too, see how it compares with yours."

Erin stood, red faced, as she turned to her neighbors and friends. "The board evaluated both proposals and thought this was the better plan." That started another argument that lasted for the next ten minutes.

Erin looked around and knew this back-and-forth helped no one.

She motioned for everyone to be quiet, and it

took a few seconds for everyone to quit talking. Traci glared at her from her second-row seat.

"I appreciate everyone's support and faith in me, but listening to my proposal won't settle anything. The board has already voted, and, after reviewing Sawyer's plan, I'd say he has a good one."

Several people started to protest, but she held up her hands. "I like his ideas on how to bring outside money to our rodeo and city. I hadn't thought about that.

"There were a couple of other ideas that surprised me, but I think they might work here. But I also have a few items that Mr. Jensen didn't think about, and I plan to suggest them to him and push to implement them." She grinned. "He won't remain unscathed."

Standing, Bob said, "You sure, Erin?"

"I am." She scanned the audience. "What we need to do is all come together and start working on the rodeo. A good idea is a good idea." She turned back to Sawyer. "No matter who came up with it."

She heard chuckles in the audience. "So, I think now that we've heard Sawyer's plan, we should get behind it and support it one hundred percent."

Melvin's mouth hung open, and his wife had to elbow him. From Traci's expression it looked as if she'd sucked a lemon, but Andy nodded to Erin.

Erin took her seat again.

Sawyer stood by the podium. "Any more questions or comments?"

The room remained quiet.

"Then I guess this meeting is over." Sawyer walked down the stage steps to the floor of the room, waiting in case anyone wanted to talk privately. No one came by. He didn't know if that was good or bad. But what he did know was Erin had stood up for him. That found a spot in his heart.

Erin's friends clustered around her, asking questions. This time, her brain had comprehended Sawyer's words, and she saw her neighbors' reactions. She'd been impressed. He'd put together a thorough plan to get their rodeo back on its feet. But she had modifications that could maximize his ideas.

As she talked with other residents, Erin saw out of the corner of her eye Sawyer packing up his laptop and projector. When he walked by Tate, her brother said something. Sawyer stopped. The two exchanged words, then Sawyer walked on.

Aunt Betty frowned and leaned close to Tate. "I may be old but..."

Erin couldn't hear the rest of what her aunt said. Tate shrugged and jogged up the other aisle out to their car.

What had that been about?

Now, several of the board members gathered in front of the stage around Sawyer. Bob joined them.

"I'm going to go through the facility tomorrow morning to do a more detailed inspection, making notes on what needs to be updated or replaced. I'd be happy to have anyone walk through with me," Sawyer announced to the room.

"I'll be there," Bob Rivera replied. "You going to notify the folks in Harding?"

"I will," Sawyer replied.

Bob nodded his approval.

Sawyer looked at Erin, silently asking if she would be there.

"You'll see me," Erin answered. She tried to keep her expression neutral, but felt a smile curve her lips.

He returned the smile, which made her heart light.

Later, when she and her aunt walked out to the car, Erin asked, "What was all that about with Tate and Sawyer earlier?"

"Your brother was just trying to give the new guy a hard time."

"What'd Tate say?"

Betty kissed Erin's cheek and opened the passenger-side door. Obviously, Auntie wasn't going to tell her.

Why?

Chapter Three

Sawyer parked his truck in front of his hotel room, grabbed his laptop and projector, and slipped out of the truck.

"Let me help you," Lencho called, walking to Sawyer's side and taking the projector.

Sawyer grabbed the key from his pocket and opened the door.

"I liked your presentation for the rodeo."

Sawyer nodded. "Good to hear."

"I did want to hear Erin's plan, and when she said it wasn't necessary, it surprised me, knowing how competitive she is." He shrugged. "But if she thought your plan was good, we can count on it." He grinned. "I know she'll give you her ideas, and she *ain't* shy about voicing her opinion."

"Really?"

Lencho opened his mouth to respond, but saw the teasing in Sawyer's face. Opening the door,

Sawyer motioned Lencho inside. The young man put the projector on the desk.

"So, you're telling me that Erin will keep me honest."

Red ran up the teen's neck. "I didn't mean it like that, but if you give her your word, you better live up to what you've said."

"Good to know."

"And it's the same with her. If she gives you her word, you can count on it. And she has another thing. It's kinda related to her first thing. Don't lie. It ain't worth it."

"So you've been on the wrong side of her?"

"Uh, kinda. But it only happened once," he quickly added. "And you always know where you stand with Erin. I like it. She's not like other girls who want to play head games."

Obviously, the young man thought the world of Erin.

"Thanks for the advice."

"No problem." He left, closing the door behind him.

Sawyer locked the door and sat down in the flowered chair by the table in the room. The meeting tonight had been much easier than he'd expected, due to Erin's intervention.

Her actions puzzled him. He knew she wanted the job, so why'd she give up so quickly? He hadn't seen her proposal, but had it been inferior to his?

That thought didn't sit well with him. So what was it?

She had cut off Bob's insistence to prolong this process. But why? What motivated her? His experience with competitors was that they didn't act out of noble purposes. So, why'd she do it?

He stood and retrieved his laptop. Before he could boot up, his phone rang.

"Hi, Sawyer, how was your first day on the job?" Caleb, his older brother, asked. "Did it go well?"

"It's been an interesting day."

"Oh? What happened?" The tone of Caleb's voice changed from teasing to serious in a heartbeat.

"There was another competitor for the job, and some of the townspeople wanted to hear her ideas. She's local talent."

"She?"

Sawyer explained the situation with Erin and her qualified support tonight. "And the final twist is that she didn't know the results of the vote until she walked into the board meeting."

"So was there a big scene?"

"No."

Both men remained silent.

"Do you think she acted that way to stay in with the rodeo redo just to make your life miserable?"

After thinking a moment, Sawyer said, "No.

She doesn't strike me as a woman with a sneaky side. So far she's been up-front and honest."

"You mean she's not trying to manipulate you like Mom?"

Sawyer thought about it. He didn't know Erin well enough, but his gut feeling told him no. "Tonight at a public meeting, she put an end to the argument about my winning."

Caleb didn't respond. Finally, he said, "Well, just watch yourself. We've been on the wrong side of people before."

"True, but enough about me, how's that wife of yours doing?" Sawyer wanted to get the topic off him and onto the new baby coming.

"She says she's okay, but she keeps puking. How could that be fine?"

Sawyer's concern spiked. "Is anything wrong?"

"Yeah. Morning sickness. She can't stand the smell of coffee anymore." The last words out of his mouth sounded strangled.

Sawyer laughed. "This is a new development."

"It is. The first time she threw up on me, I thought it a fluke. But time two and three, we knew.

"Herbal tea. She wants me to drink herbal tea. Have you ever tasted that stuff? Looks like dishwater and smells about as bad. I've seen stagnant creeks I'd drink out of before the stuff she's drinking."

"It's a small price to pay for me having a niece

or a nephew." Sawyer wanted to laugh again, but took pity on his brother.

"Are you going to give up coffee to support me?" Caleb demanded.

"Nope. So what are you doing about it?"

"Running to the barn where Gramps brews a pot of coffee. Brenda knows what we're doing and stays away until ten. I'm wondering if I'll live through this."

Sawyer had to laugh. "You'll live."

Caleb mumbled something.

"You're going to have to gut it up, brother."

"That's what Gramps says, but I don't know if he knows what he's talking about. Do you know how many things could go wrong?"

"Trust him. He's seen his children and grand-children born. He knows more than us. And Brenda being Brenda, if something's wrong, she'll see about it. Is she going to quit going to school?"

"No."

The quickness of his brother's answer told him that Caleb had made the mistake of asking his wife the same question. Sawyer grinned. "If she doesn't think she's in danger, then relax. I think your wife wants you to unwind and help her."

"If you say so, but I want you to be careful about the woman you told me about."

"Will do. Let me know how things are there." Sawyer hung up and sat staring at his computer.

Caleb thought Erin had another agenda. He'd have to be on his guard against her no matter how strangely his heart reacted to the woman. But there was still something about Erin Delong that he was missing. What?

The next morning, Erin arrived at the rodeo grounds before any other board member. She parked by Sawyer's truck, took the last swig of her coffee and got out.

"Ah, a lady who likes her coffee," Sawyer commented as he walked toward her.

"Guilty as charged. I haven't met a cowboy who doesn't run on it." She placed her travel mug in the center console between the front seats and closed the door.

"True." He shifted, then smiled at her. "I wanted to thank you for your words of support last night."

She nodded. "But, as I told Bob, I plan to have my say if I see things that need to be done." She had relived that meeting multiple times after she got home, checking whether she'd missed anything. The man seemed to rattle her thinking processes, leaving her to wonder if she'd lost her edge. Usually, she found it easy to cut through to the heart of the matter or see what drove a person. With Sawyer, she felt blind, groping in the dark. He made her feel nervous and off-balance.

And what her senses told her, she didn't believe, which was a first for her.

"I'd expect nothing less." He nodded to her, but there was something else in his eyes that she couldn't nail down. Was that humor? Interest?

Before she could respond, Mel drove into the parking lot, followed by several other board members in their vehicles. Five minutes later, Harding County board members arrived. Bob Rivera also appeared. "Morning."

They walked through the empty rodeo grounds discussing Sawyer's plan and other concerns the board members had. Bob hung back and observed the tour.

"Who do you have a contract with to provide the rides?" Sawyer asked Mel as they stood in the empty area where the rides would be located.

Mel named the company they'd used previously to provide the carnival rides for the rodeo.

Sawyer frowned. "I wouldn't use them this year. I have the names of a couple of different vendors."

"Why?" Chris Saddler asked. "We've worked with that company for years."

Erin could always count on Chris to bring up questions she had. When Chris asked a question of Mel, he got answers. When she asked a question on the same subject, Mel gave her nothing but grief.

"The company you're using had a lawsuit filed

against them last week, and their safety record is iffy," Sawyer answered.

The board members all looked at Mel.

"Did you know about their history?" Norman asked.

"This is the first I've heard of this."

Erin kept her mouth shut but met Mel's gaze. She and her dad had argued with him about the company, but he had pushed aside their concerns.

Mel ground his teeth and turned to face Sawyer. "I've heard rumors. We can look into your suggestions," he said reluctantly.

As they finished the tour of the grounds, Mel did a good imitation of a petulant child, with his stomping feet and bad attitude. The other board members grew uncomfortable with his actions.

"I think half these vendor booths should be offered to people in Harding," Norman stated.

"And if there are not enough people in Harding who want to pay for one of the booths, offer the rest of the booths to anyone in the state who wants to rent them," Erin added.

"Good idea," Bob Rivera said.

The others agreed.

"Okay, I can get those contracts reviewed and awarded," Sawyer added.

The group started toward their cars. Mel stepped closer to Sawyer. "You were hired for your talent and not anyone else's." Mel glared at Erin.

"So does that mean you don't want me to consider any of the suggestions from the other rodeo board members that vary from the original contract?" Sawyer spoke loudly enough for everyone to hear. "And does that warning include you?"

Everyone stopped.

Mel glanced around, then swallowed. "No, that's not what I meant."

"Good, because if any of the local residents or board members know of a way to cut costs to bring us in under budget, I want to know." Sawyer turned to the others. "I'll email updates weekly to the board members and have the changes posted at the rodeo office."

The members nodded and walked to their cars.

Mel shot Erin a last disgruntled look and trudged to his truck.

Bob waited behind with Erin and Sawyer. "Well, Mr. Jensen, you just got on Mel's bad side."

"Could be."

"Thankfully, you were already awarded the contract," Bob added.

"True, but once the project gets started, Mel will change his mind."

"Don't count on it." Bob nodded to Erin and Sawyer and walked away.

Erin stood there absorbing Sawyer's defense of her. It was the last thing she had expected from him, but there it was, warming her heart. It was something not a lot of people did for her. They always expected her to be the strong one, defending others. To be on the receiving end of it was like a gentle rain on her parched soul. "Thanks for your support." Erin didn't know how to handle this man. Too often, other professional men not from around here approached her ideas with skepticism. He didn't seem fazed by her suggestions but, instead, welcomed them.

He nodded. "I liked your idea to make sure all the booths were occupied."

Oddly, she wanted to preen over his compliment. "It's just common sense."

His rich laughter filled the air. "Sometimes common sense is the last thing that rules."

"True."

"I'm heading back to the rodeo office to go over the books for the last few years. I could use help from someone familiar with what's gone on before, and a board member would be perfect for the job."

The offer only added to her confused reaction to him. "I've got the morning free, so I can do that."

"Good."

They walked to their trucks.

"Growing up, I spent a lot of time on these grounds. I looked forward to September when the rodeo came," Erin said.

"I understand. Summers my brother and I followed the traveling rodeo wherever it went."

"What'd your parents think of that?"

His expression slammed shut, throwing her back on her heels. "My father died when I was young."

The tone of his voice didn't encourage any other questions. "I'm sorry." Erin didn't push. "I'll see you at the offices." She opened the door of her truck and slid into the driver's seat.

Pulling out of the parking lot, she glanced in her rearview mirror and saw Sawyer standing by his truck, studying her.

"I guess he thought I might get into his business. Too bad the man doesn't know me," she said out loud. A smile slowly curved her lips. "But he'll learn."

When Sawyer walked into the offices of the bicounty rodeo, Erin sat talking to the secretary.

"I appreciate your prayers, Lisa. Dad's improving a little each day."

The women stopped and looked at him.

"Did you get lost?" Erin asked, her voice light.

"No, but I drove through the rodeo grounds and confirmed that the back entrance to the grounds needs the road widened and marked."

"Excellent idea," Erin replied.

Lisa grinned.

"What?" Sawyer looked at both women.

"Erin proposed that last year, but Mel disagreed and wouldn't bring it up at the board meeting."

"Well, I agree with you."

"Good to know."

"Let's move into the other room and start working on this rodeo."

A small office stood behind the reception area. Down from the office was a meeting room where Sawyer and Erin could spread out. On one side of the room were bookshelves filled with binders of past rodeos. The notebooks went back to 1937.

"I see this rodeo has a long past." Sawyer nodded to the notebooks. "It's great it's been documented."

Erin pulled the first notebook off the shelf. Carefully, she put the binder on the table, opened it and slowly turned the pages.

Looking over her shoulder, Sawyer read the name of Clayton Delong. He stepped closer. "Clayton Delong? Is he related to you?"

She looked up. Suddenly, the air between them thickened with awareness. Her eyes drifted toward his mouth. Swallowing, she said, "He was my dad's grandfather. The rodeo has always been connected with my family, but as time has gone on, others in the community have bought in. When our rodeo combined with the Harding County rodeo, the Delong share diminished, but Dad still sits on the board."

Her interest in the rodeo suddenly took on a different dimension. This was family heritage. He could respect that and admire it, but he hoped he'd read her right and she'd work to make this redo a success and not want to make it about the Delong name. So far, she'd indicated she wanted the rodeo's success, but he'd been fooled before, so he knew not to let his heart lead the way. That didn't stop his heart from pounding at her nearness. He was here only to fix the rodeo, nothing more.

He swallowed the lump in his throat. "So this is in your blood."

"It is. But since the rodeo merged with the Harding County one, our family has not been as involved. Plus, I've been away at school and competing in barrel racing on weekends elsewhere, so I've not been here. Dad's called me and told me about the problems, but that's ancient history. Let's talk about your plan and how to implement it. And, if it needs to be tweaked, we can see about that."

Well, if he thought she'd back off, he realized he was mistaken. But he wasn't fazed in the least.

She opened the massive tote she had with her and pulled out his proposal, a notebook and several pens, setting them on the table. "I'm ready."

He knew a challenge when he saw one. "Let me get my papers."

She smiled in a way that indicated this wasn't going to be easy. She would have her say. When he walked back into the room, he had his notebooks and her proposal.

She pointed to her proposal. "Why do you have that?"

"I found it in here when I was looking for the financial records for the losing years of the rodeo, and I wanted to read it."

"And?"

"I thought you had some good ideas, so let's discuss how we can incorporate them into my plan."

The corners of her mouth curled up. "Did you find the records for last year?"

"No, and I'd like to see those, to find out where the money was spent."

"My father, as a board member, has a copy of those records, but they're at home."

Erin stood and walked out to Lisa's desk in the reception area. "Do you know where the financial records are for the past several years?" Sawyer heard Erin ask.

"They are in Mel's office."

"Could we see them for the last year?"

"Sure, I'll get them."

Erin appeared back in the boardroom. Before they could get started, Lisa stood in the doorway. "Those records are not in Mel's office. I have last year's numbers on a flash drive in my desk. I'll bring it to you."

Several minutes later she reappeared. "I can't find the flash drive, either. It's not in my desk."

Sawyer met Erin's gaze.

"Lisa, that's okay," Erin reassured her. "If you find either the hard copy or your flash drive, let us know."

Once they were alone, Sawyer said, "That doesn't speak well of the record keeping around here."

Erin shook her head. "It's not Lisa's fault."

"Then where are the documents?"

"You'll need to talk to Mel. He's the one in charge."

So Mel was in charge of the documentation? The only reason Sawyer could think of everything disappearing was that Mel had something to hide.

For the balance of the morning, Erin and Sawyer went over his proposal page by page as they sat in the conference room. Erin wanted to understand his thinking and how he planned to execute his ideas. She'd prepared herself to argue her viewpoint, but much to her surprise, Sawyer didn't discount her opinion. He listened to her suggestions, considered modifying his plans, questioned her reasoning, then they came to a consensus. She welcomed his reasonable reaction, so different from Mel and some of the other men she'd dealt with in town.

"So, are you using some of the local residents in this rebuilding?" Erin asked.

"Is there a cement contractor in town?"

He knew there wasn't but wanted to make his point.

"No, we both know that, but there are local artisans who are excellent welders, and iron workers who know how to make the rodeo grounds more appealing for the visitors and horses. They could do some of the smaller projects. They'd welcome the work, and their hearts would be in the game."

Leaning back in his chair, he studied her. "I had planned on using larger companies out of Albuquerque for the main infrastructure components. But I'd like to encourage local craftsmen to bid on some of the smaller projects. I thought I'd add to the rodeo web page a list of the jobs that need to be done." Sawyer picked up his pen and tapped it against the table. "I have a budget I need to stick to, Erin. I don't think the board wants any overruns."

He had a valid point.

"But you might not reach all the local craftsmen. One of the local iron workers refuses to use the internet."

"So, if I wanted to advertise for local iron workers and other people to hire, where would I do that?"

She blinked. Her mind had geared up to argue for the local residents, and he'd short-circuited her brain. Again.

The glint in his eyes caught her attention. "Bob

Rivera is the man who knows everyone in this county and the surrounding counties. We could walk down to his store and ask him. Or, better yet, we could list the jobs, post it in his store and ask for bids. It's not modern and high-tech, but some of the artisans prefer face-to-face business deals."

"I like that idea. Why don't we make that list, then go over to Bob's and post it? The sooner we fill the contracts, the sooner we get to work."

For the next few minutes they worked on Sawyer's laptop creating the job list. She'd been impressed he didn't ask the secretary or her to do it, but did it himself. Too often, she'd seen the guy in charge think the underlings should do the work.

"I should've had you type my econ paper." She laughed. "You're faster than I am. I flunked keyboarding in school and did the hunt and peck method my dad does. Why, even Tate is faster than me."

He chuckled, then saved the file and hit Print. Then he walked to Lisa's desk and waited for the printer to spit out the list, but nothing happened.

He quickly jotted down the jobs on a piece of paper.

"You did notice that I recommended the first thing they spend money on was a new computer and printer," Erin commented.

"I did. That will be one of the first purchases I make." He closed his laptop and notebooks and put them back in his office.

A glow of pride shot through her.

"Remember what I told the other board members? A good idea is a good idea no matter who suggests it. I don't have a corner on the market."

As they walked down the street to Bob's hardware store, people came out of the buildings, seemingly curious. "Come see," Erin answered. The people followed behind. Erin heard murmured comments.

When they entered the hardware store, Bob and Tom Kirby, a local rancher, were at the checkout counter talking.

"Morin', Erin." He looked at Sawyer and nodded.

"Is there something I can help you with?" Bob asked.

Erin heard the other residents filing into the building.

"Sawyer and I have been discussing the rodeo redo and how to implement it. Sawyer needs the names of local vendors who want to bid on working for the rodeo."

"Oh?" Bob frowned at Sawyer. "I thought he'd want to use the big boys out of Albuquerque."

"I'm open to all bids. I do have a budget, but I want to include as many local vendors as possible. They know the history of the rodeo, and that could put a different spin on the work they do."

Bob considered Sawyer's words. He turned to Erin, silently asking if she believed this stranger.

"I think it's a good idea, Bob," she replied. "Locals would have a shot at working on the rodeo. It would give them a personal stake in the project and an opportunity to show off their work and maybe get other contracts."

"I think so, too," came a shouted reply from the back. "I'd be interested," a man called out.

Erin looked over her shoulder at the man who'd offered the comment and gave him a thumbs-up.

"Okay, give me the list of what you need, and I'll post it in the store. The folks behind you will read it and spread the word."

They didn't need the internet in this town. Word of mouth was faster and the mode that had been used for over a hundred years, but Sawyer wanted to use the internet to bring younger people into the redo.

Sawyer pulled a slip of paper out of his shirt pocket and placed it on the counter. "Anyone who wants to bid can come by the rodeo board office." Sawyer turned to the group. "So read the list and, if you have any of the skills needed, come by and talk to me, then put in your bid."

Sawyer and Erin made their way through the crowd by the front door, leaving Bob and Tom with their mouths hanging open.

Erin laughed.

"What's so funny?" Sawyer asked.

"I don't think I've seen Bob that off-balance before."

"I do have that effect on people."

Boy, didn't she know it. No matter how much she wanted to dislike him for getting the job she'd thought was hers, he managed to throw something in her way that made it impossible.

"C'mon, Auntie, we're late," Erin said, trying to speed up her aunt and brother as they walked into the Hope Community Church.

"I'm not the one who caused the delay." Betty eyed her nephew. "What was Tate thinking about, wearing his torn cutoffs and old plaid slip-on tennis shoes with holes in each shoe to church?"

When Tate had appeared in the kitchen for breakfast, Auntie had sent him back to his room to change before he could touch any of the food. She'd ended her scolding with the threat that he had five minutes before she threw his breakfast in the garbage. Tate made it back in time to eat his egg-and-bacon flat-bread sandwich.

Entering the church, people clustered in different spots in the main sanctuary talking. They turned and acknowledged Erin and the family.

From the instant Bob had posted the jobs that needed to be filled, a constant stream of residents had come by the hardware store and rodeo board's headquarters. The board members in Harding County got the word that they were hiring for jobs to work on the rodeo. People had called and stopped by the Delong home to check out the rumors about jobs working on the rodeo. It'd been the talk of the town. No, it had been the talk of the county, and late Saturday night some jobs had appeared on the website.

As Betty, Tate and Erin made their way to the front left side of the church, their regular place, several people stopped and chatted about the rumblings in the county and asked about Erin's dad. Finally, Tate threw up his hands and just walked on and sat where he normally sat.

When the organist slipped behind her instrument and started to play, people took their seats. The pastor welcomed everyone and announced the hymns for the morning. After they finished the first hymn, someone slid into the pew beside her. When Erin looked over, Sawyer stood there. He winked and started singing the second hymn.

The man had a marvelous baritone voice that flowed around her, making her just want to sit down and listen to him sing. Auntie looked around Erin and smiled at him. Erin felt a dozen different people staring at them.

She didn't want to be the center of attention, but apparently she was.

The pastor announced upcoming church events and welcomed Sawyer to the service. He also prayed for those with needs, updating the congregation on Detrick's condition and asking God for a speedy recovery.

What the pastor preached on, she had no idea. All she could think about was the man sitting beside her.

Before the final amen faded away, they were surrounded by members of the congregation. Everyone wanted to meet the new guy in town. Pastor Antonio "Tony" Hooper walked over and introduced himself.

"I'm glad you decided to join us for church this morning. You are welcome."

The people around them agreed.

"Well, I wanted to find a church, since I'm going to be here a few months."

Respect filled Tony's gaze. "I'm glad to hear that. We are also grateful for the jobs coming into the county. And with you posting them at the hardware store, everyone knows about the opportunities."

"I'll credit Erin with that. It was her suggestion to make sure the local artisans and workers were given the opportunity to work for the rodeo."

"Well, that doesn't surprise me. Erin's always

thinking about the people around here." Pastor patted Erin on the back.

"I'm hungry, Aunt Betty," Tate said loud enough to stop all conversation.

Uncomfortable chuckles floated through the room.

Betty looked at Tate, then Sawyer. "No doubt we're all hungry. Sawyer, come to the house and have lunch with us."

"I wouldn't want to put you out, Betty," Sawyer replied.

She waved away his comment. "I always fix too much since I'm used to cooking for eight people. Tate eats enough for two, and, although Erin has a healthy appetite, I'll have leftovers. And it will help your budget since, knowing Mel, I'm sure your meal allowance isn't that much."

"For sure," someone whispered.

Sawyer looked as if he fought a grin. "Betty, you've got me."

She nodded her head. "Follow us out to the ranch."

As Sawyer walked from the church, Traci appeared in front of him. From the look on her face, she had heard what Betty said. "Surely, you're not going to eat with them."

Traci could be heard plainly throughout the parking lot.

"It would be ungracious for me to not show up since I've already accepted Betty's invitation."

Traci stepped closer and whispered something in his ear.

Taking a step backward, he smiled. "I look forward to it."

Traci glanced at Erin, gave her a cat-who-ate-the-canary smile and sauntered to her car. Sawyer walked to his own vehicle, parked not far from Erin's. Betty and Tate sat in the car. "What took you so long?"

He looked over his shoulder at Traci. "I tried to dodge a bullet but ran into a tree."

Erin knew exactly what he meant. She snorted. "I'll see you at the house."

As he followed her out of the parking lot, she laughed softly.

"That girl doesn't know when to quit," Betty mumbled.

"I know, Auntie, but you got to him first."

Betty nodded. "You can count on me."

"No truer words were ever spoken, Auntie."

Chapter Four

"He's still following you, Daughter."

Erin jerked her gaze away from the rearview mirror to her aunt. Erin simply shrugged and didn't defend herself.

"Are you upset that I invited him to lunch?" A satisfied smile curled Auntie's mouth.

Betty had never met a stranger without always feeling it her duty to feed them. "No, just surprised, since he won the contract over me, remember?"

"You're beyond that and already challenging him. Bob's wife told me about what happened yesterday. Little did he expect you to voice your opinions so quickly, but you have. Has he objected? Been unkind? Overbearing?"

Looking in the rearview mirror, Erin saw Tate roll his eyes.

"No, he hasn't. But—" She needed to quit while she was ahead.

Betty waited. "But what?"

"He read my proposal for updating the rodeo." All yesterday Erin thought about Sawyer, trying to sort out her conflicting emotions toward him. After another long ride on Wind Dancer, Erin knew her heart was involved.

Betty turned to her, her eyes wide and her mouth pursed into an O. "And?"

"He likes some of my ideas and wants to incorporate them, particularly my ideas for the midway."

Her aunt nodded. "A reasonable man. Good."

"But we've discovered a problem."

Betty frowned. "Oh?"

"The final figures for the last year are missing. We asked Lisa about them, but she couldn't find them. She had copies in several different places but couldn't find any of them."

The ranch house appeared, cutting off their conversation. The low-slung house and barn sat back off the road. When her great-grandfather had built the house and out structures, he'd used adobe, just as the natives of the area did. It had caused a stir among some of his friends but, during the hot summers, their home became the place where everyone met.

The driveway sat between the house and the barn with a covered breezeway connecting the kitchen door to the barn's side door. Beyond that, several corrals had been set up for Erin to practice her barrel racing. Her truck and horse trailer sat on the far side of the drive.

Erin parked next to the kitchen door.

Sawyer pulled in beside her and hurried out of his truck. He opened Betty's door and helped her out.

"Thank you." Betty glowed like a schoolgirl.

Tate clambered out of the backseat and slammed his door. He ignored everyone, walking inside. Sawyer's gaze roamed over the house, barn and corrals.

"Tate and Erin's great-grandfather built this place," Betty explained.

"Auntie, Sawyer's not interested in ancient history."

"No, I love to hear family histories," Sawyer replied.

Really? That was hard to believe. He'd be the first man she'd run into with that attitude. "Well, we better get inside. With the mood Tate is in, who knows what he's doing. When I suggested driving to see Dad this morning, Tate didn't want to go." It only had been three days since she'd returned to Tucumcari, but she was willing to make another trip to Albuquerque if her brother wanted to visit the hospital.

"You're right." Betty hurried into the kitchen.

Sawyer stopped on the step up to the back door and scanned the yard. "Your family's got a nice setup here."

Erin picked up the tinge of sadness, or maybe it was longing in his voice. "Thanks. I miss this place when I'm away. There's a unique beauty in the starkness that calls to your soul." She shrugged. "I'll admit, it doesn't call to everyone, but for me, it—" She broke off and glanced up at him, expecting to see disdain, but instead she found understanding.

"I can see that." He opened his mouth to say more but shook his head and walked into the house, leaving her unsettled because she knew he understood her.

That had never happened before.

Betty spread a feast before him of a roast, beans, bread and local greens.

"You weren't kidding, Betty," Sawyer commented as they walked into the dining room. The room had French doors that opened out onto a patio, giving them a view of the horizon.

"My job is to feed others." Her simple statement reinforced her actions of putting out a big meal. "Didn't your mother do that, too?"

The innocent question from Betty felt like a right fist to his jaw, making him step back. Sawyer looked around to see if Betty or Erin had noticed his reaction. With all their preparations, they hadn't, but Tate had.

Sawyer searched for an appropriate response. He couldn't very well say when his mother wasn't drunk or feeling sorry for herself she couldn't manage to heat up a can of soup. They didn't need to know his past. "Mom wasn't the cook you are."

Betty stopped and her gaze caught him. He tried not to reveal anything, but her expression softened and she nodded at him.

After they prayed over the food, dishes were passed around. They discussed the morning sermon and how to live it.

Finally, Erin asked, "Did Uncle complain about you leaving?"

"No, he knows better. When his sister needed me to take care of her family, I went every time I was needed." She leaned over the table. "Uncle didn't protest then. There's food in the freezer, which he could live on for months, and if he didn't want that, there are neighbors around us who would make sure he's fed." Betty smiled. "The man won't go hungry."

"I remember the first time our parents took us to Aunt Betty's," Erin said, glancing at Sawyer. "Her kitchen is the biggest room in her house, and it's the busiest, with people coming and going.

"Tate wasn't interested in the crowd in the kitchen and found the big-screen TV in the sewing room."

Sawyer smiled, enjoying the light banter among the family. Good memories.

"That's where she made Uncle put the TV," Tate explained.

"If we had to have that fancy big-screen TV and not some normal one," Betty replied, "then I was going to make Uncle put it in my sewing room so I could watch it, too, while I sewed."

"Why Uncle let you put it there—" Tate shook his head.

"He got his TV, didn't he?"

Tate shrugged and tried to suppress his smile.

"And the other boys in the neighborhood came and sat in that sewing room. They knew no shame."

"I'm surprised you let Peter and Sam Running Bear inside your house after they tried to push Tate and me down the mountain," Erin added.

Betty's eyes narrowed. "I told those boys if they ever tried that stunt again, they would never be allowed in my house to watch the big-screen TV or have fried bread."

Tate's features hardened. "You didn't need to fight my battles, Auntie. I can fight my own." He stood and stomped out of the kitchen, leaving the other three people staring at one another. Betty shook her head.

Sawyer could identify with the teen's moodiness. He stood and helped clear the table. "I wish I could've eaten more, but I didn't want to waddle to my truck."

"Don't worry." Erin put the bowl of fried bread on the counter. She pulled out freezer bags and began to put the excess food into them. "We'll either share it with others in the community or freeze it. Auntie has a reputation for feeding any-one who shows up at her door."

Sawyer stopped and studied Betty, wishing she could've been close when he and his brother needed someone like her. She returned his gaze with a penetrating one, then grabbed the bag of flat bread and shoved it at him. "For later."

At some level, he knew the older woman sensed the pain of his past. He'd known hunger. "You're doing good work."

Betty ducked her head. "There are too many people going without. My husband always had a job and we were blessed. I can do no less than share with others."

"And change lives," Sawyer murmured. "Thank you, ladies, for the meal. Now I need to go back and work." He paused. "Are your dad's notebooks here?"

"Yes, they're in the library."

"Think they might have the final numbers in them?"

"I don't know, but we should look."

He followed her to the library. She pulled down last year's notebook and handed it to him. They settled on the love seat and looked over the figures.

"These don't look like the final numbers," Sawyer commented.

Studying the final lines, Erin knew they weren't. "I agree. These look like working numbers." She glanced up into his face, realizing how close they were. She swallowed and his gaze didn't leave her face. "I'll look around to see if Dad has an addendum with the final figures." She closed the notebook and jumped up, feeling like a jack-in-the-box.

He slowly came to his feet, fighting a smile.

What was so funny, she wanted to ask, but she knew. Acting like a fifteen-year-old, which wasn't something she had done—until now.

"I'll have a listing of big contractors I need to call tomorrow. If you drop in, you can see who's shown interest in bidding."

"What time?"

"Let's try nine."

"I'll be there."

He nodded and left the room, leaving Erin clutching the notebook and feeling lost.

As Sawyer walked to his truck, he caught a glimpse of Tate disappearing into the barn.

"Tate, got a moment?" Sawyer called and waited for the teen. When Tate reappeared, the cautious expression on his face warned Sawyer to proceed carefully. "I hope I didn't barge in and ruin your Sunday lunch."

"Nah."

"I didn't mean for your sister to bring up those old stories."

"She's only a girl, and girls like to embarrass people."

Tread carefully, he warned himself. "You know

what I think? Your sister remembers that time with laughter and joy. Both your aunt and sister are strong women."

Tate cocked his head. "They want to tell me what to do all the time. They think they're always right."

"True, but girls do that. It seems to me Betty was only defending her nephew. Maybe she went about it the wrong way, but sometimes we do wrong in trying to do right. I think they're acting out of love." He smiled. "I'd give them a break."

Tate shrugged. "If you say so."

"I guess when you've been raised by a mom who was afraid of making a decision, who needed someone to make up her mind for her, it's refreshing to meet a woman who can make a decision for herself."

Tate stared at him.

Sawyer wanted to snatch the words back. Tate didn't need his lecture. Sawyer nodded and slipped into his truck. As he drove away, Sawyer saw Tate standing in the driveway, staring at him.

Well, Tate wasn't the only one who was surprised. At lunch, sitting by Erin and across from Betty, Sawyer had found himself admiring them. From the conversation, he knew Betty felt a need to feed the hungry. He admired a heart so open that she'd feed anyone who walked through her door. Betty reminded him of the church people who'd housed and fed Caleb and him in Plainview.

Caleb and he had escaped an abusive home situation. After his father died, his mother turned into a helpless woman who went from boyfriend to boyfriend. The situation went from bad to worse until Caleb was finally declared an emancipated minor and moved out, taking Sawyer with him. The brothers moved to a little town in the Texas Panhandle, where the congregation adopted them.

Tate may have complained that the women in his life were suffocating him, but the teen didn't know how good he had it.

Monday morning Sawyer and Erin went over the bids that needed to be let.

The door to the boardroom opened and Mel stood there, looking like an angry bear.

"What's going on here?" He glared at Erin.

She opened her mouth to respond, but Sawyer replied, "We're working on plans for the rodeo. Would you like to join us in our session?"

Mel's jaw flexed. "No. That's why you were hired, but what is she doing here?"

"Didn't you read the email that Sawyer sent out last night?" Erin asked. "He invited any of the board members to the meeting this morning to get their input."

"Erin was the only one to show up this morning. I needed someone familiar with the area and people. She's helped with the logistics."

Mel didn't reply but turned to leave.

"Mel," Sawyer called out, "I wanted to see the final figures for the last year, to help improve the bidding, but I haven't found those records. Didn't Lisa contact you?"

Mel's back stiffened. "There are books here with the budgets in them."

"But the final ones are nowhere to be found," Sawyer replied. "The backup ones on the flash drives are missing, too, so I wondered if you have another copy somewhere."

"I do. At home, but Erin's father should have copies of them, too, for the last few years since he was on the board."

"We looked for those figures yesterday," Erin informed him, "but only found working numbers. After I went through the notebook a second time, I found a note Dad scribbled inside that you'd provide the final numbers after the rodeo."

Mel's jaw flexed. "I'll bring the notebook by tomorrow before I drive to Las Vegas to meet with some of the board members out of Harding County. Is there anything else you need?"

"Las Vegas?" Sawyer asked, puzzled.

"Our Vegas, in San Miguel County," Erin supplied. "Our city is older than the Vegas in Nevada and dates back to 1835."

"Maybe the board should've gone with the person who knew this area," Mel grumbled. He eyed Erin.

Sawyer straightened his shoulders. Mel's words hit Sawyer wrong. Giving one's word meant the world to him. His mother's word changed with the wind or her feelings, and nothing that she promised or said could be counted on. "Feel free to revisit the decision to hire me, Mel. Let me know later today of your verdict. But realize you'll need a cause for the dismissal."

"I know the contract."

Mel stalked out.

Silence settled over the room.

"I'm sorry I didn't tell you about the note I found."

Sawyer studied the notebook in front of him, then looked up. "Not a problem."

Erin lifted her pen and tapped it against the table. "When you get on the wrong side of Mel, well, life's not pleasant. The board made a decision and while I would've loved to have gotten the contract, we need to stick with what we did. The county can't move with Mel's moods."

"Or his daughter's."

Erin bit her lip to keep from smiling. Sawyer grinned. She gave in and they laughed.

Sharing the humorous moment softened Erin's heart more.

"Don't worry. There's lots going on right now."

Before she could reply, her cell phone rang. She pulled it from her purse.

"Erin, this is Sheriff Trujillo."

Her heart nearly stopped. "Sheriff? Why are you calling?"

Sawyer's attention shifted to her.

"I have Tate here at the jail. I talked with your aunt and she said you were in town."

"What happened?"

"One of the deputies found him out at the rodeo grounds, racing around the parking lot. We nabbed him. You need to come by the jail and get him."

"I can be there in less than five minutes. I'm at the rodeo board office, working."

"Then I'll see you in a few minutes." He hung up.

Erin slowly put her phone on the table.

"What's wrong?" Sawyer asked.

Taking a deep breath, she looked at him. "My brother skipped school, and one of the deputies caught him at the rodeo grounds and brought him to the jail to cool his heels until a family member can come by and get him."

"Is he under arrest?"

"No, but I need to go see about it." She stood and threw everything in her purse.

"What are you going to do?"

"Other than strangle him?"

"That probably won't be helpful," Sawyer added.

"True, but what was he thinking of, skipping school?"

"He might be hurting and, being a teenage boy, he doesn't know how to reach out."

Sawyer's quiet explanation stopped her cold. He had a point. She knew her brother hurt, as demonstrated by his outburst on Sunday. She'd asked Tate later that day about the incident at lunch, but he'd refused to talk about the problem.

"So what do you suggest?"

"Well, since you won't be able to drive both yours and Tate's trucks, I could ride with Tate to the high school and we have a little boy talk. Afterward, I could drive back here with you."

"What if he doesn't want to talk?"

"Then we drive back in silence. It won't bother me, but your brother might feel more comfortable talking to another male."

The ring of truth in his suggestion convinced her. "Okay, let's go."

It took seven minutes to get to the jail. As they walked into the office, Sawyer whispered, "Keep cool. You might want to yell at your brother, but don't. You can yell at me later."

She hated to admit it, but Sawyer's perspective made sense. Clamping down on her emotions, she saw Tate sitting on the bench against the wall. His head jerked up when he saw her and Sawyer. Immediately, his slouchy posture disappeared and he sat up straight. He expected her to rain down on him, but Sawyer's words rang in her ears.

The sheriff appeared from around the corner

where the cells were located. "Sorry to have to call you, Erin, with all that's happening in your family, but the deputy came across your brother doing wheelies in the rodeo parking lot and making such a racket with those pipes on his truck that I'm surprised the sheriff in the next county didn't catch him."

Tate's chin jutted out.

The sheriff stood in front of Tate. "So should I issue him a ticket for the illegal tailpipes on his truck, or you can make sure he gets back to school and I'll ignore those pipes for the moment?"

Tate wasn't the first teenager the sheriff had scared straight.

They looked at Tate.

"What do you want to do?" Erin asked. She had plenty of words and thoughts she wanted to share but battled her natural urges.

After a moment, Tate said, "I'll go back to school."

"And stay there," the sheriff added.

"Yeah, I'll stay in school."

"Okay," the sheriff said, "but those pipes will have to be fixed if you want to drive your truck anyplace other than the racetrack. Understood?" Turning to Erin, he added, "I think you should take away your brother's truck for a while."

Tate's expression turned to stone.

"I'd skip making him walk to school like my

father did me," the sheriff added, his tone light, "but there should be consequences."

He returned Tate's keys and billfold, which had been taken when the teen was picked up, and the trio walked out of the jail. They crowded into Erin's truck.

Tate sat between Erin and Sawyer. "What are you doing here?" Tate snapped at Sawyer.

"That's enough," Erin replied, wanting to add that it was *his*, not Sawyer's, bad behavior that had caused the mess, but she felt Sawyer's gaze on her, helping her control her reaction.

"I'm here to help your sister with how we get you back to school," Sawyer calmly answered.

"I can drive myself."

"True, but can I trust you, Tate?" Erin replied, fighting for an even tone. "How good is your word that you'll drive back to school? As good as your promise to go to school this morning?"

Outrage and shame radiated in waves off the youth.

Sawyer caught Erin's gaze and shook his head, reminding her not to be too harsh on her brother.

Silence reigned in the truck as they drove the rest of the way to the rodeo grounds. She stopped by the only truck in the parking lot. The boys slipped out.

"I'll follow you," Erin called out as Tate stood by the driver's door of his truck.

Her brother nodded and slipped inside.

Sawyer looked at Erin. "You did good back there with your brother." He reached out and squeezed her hand. Turning, he raced to Tate's truck. Moisture gathered in her eyes. He had seen both Tate's and her needs and met them. She didn't know whether to treasure the experience or be frightened of it. But she could get used to having him around.

Tate put the keys in the ignition.

Sawyer buckled his seat belt, then leaned back. "I'm ready."

Tate gunned the engine.

"I'd be careful. Why bring wrath down on your head if you don't have to?"

Tate glared at Sawyer but glanced in the rear-view mirror. One look was all it took. He put the truck in gear and started driving at a normal speed.

After a moment of silence, Tate growled, "You going to lecture me about ditching?"

Sawyer recognized a youth spoiling for a fight. "Nope."

Tate's body relaxed. "So, why are you here? Because I don't need a babysitter."

"True. I'm here because your sister needed some help making sure you get back to school. She might think she can tackle anything, but driving two trucks at the same time is something even she can't do."

Tate snorted and glanced at him. "There are some things Sis can't do. Besides, I could've driven myself and she could've followed."

"True, but what if you just took off on Route 66? Could she have stopped you?"

"I told her I'd go back and—" Tate swallowed hard.

Tate's reaction told Sawyer he'd made his point. "You have to admit Erin has a lot on her plate right now. Your dad, the rodeo and you. We all need help at some time."

"That's just a line," Tate snapped, his defensiveness rising.

"Not for me. I've been there. Needed help, and I got it."

"You're just saying that." Tate kept his eyes on the road.

"Nope. When I was fourteen and my brother sixteen, he took over the role of parent."

"Why?"

"My dad died of a heart attack, and my mom couldn't cope with the situation."

Tate didn't ask any follow-up questions. He wasn't at a place to trust a stranger, and Sawyer understood that.

After several moments, Sawyer asked, "I have a question for you. Is your sister as good as she claims to be? Is she reliable? We're working on the rodeo, and I want to know if I can rely on her to do what she says she'll do."

The youth's attitude changed. "Yeah. You can count on her. She's good. If you ask her to do something, you don't ever have to think about it again. She doesn't need a reminder. She gets kinda insulted if you do." He grinned. "When she focuses on a job, she won't quit until it's finished. She focuses so hard that she sometimes forgets the small stuff. I remember one time she walked through the kitchen without her shoes and probably would've left without them. Mom stopped her before she got out of the house. But, I'll admit, she's a little off on the small details. Mom calls it Erin's walking-in-the-clouds thinking mode. Erin sees the big picture."

"So you would depend on her?"

"In a heartbeat."

Sawyer nodded. "Good. I'll trust her, but you might try trusting her, too."

Tate's shoulders tightened, telling Sawyer his words had hit the mark.

To ease the tension between them, Sawyer asked, "Do you know anywhere around here where I could rent a horse and ride? Riding helps me to clear my head. I left my horse at my brother's ranch, so when I go home, I ride as much as I can."

"You can come out to our place and ride anytime you want. I like riding, too."

"You sure?"

"Yeah. Dad's horse is going to need to be ridden, so come and exercise Duke."

"Duke?"

Tate shrugged, trying to be cool, but the smile dancing around his mouth gave him away. "Dad loved John Wayne, so in honor of him, Dad named his horse Duke."

They pulled into the high school parking lot and Tate found a spot.

"Thanks for the invite to ride. I hope you'll think about what I said about your sister."

Tate studied him and nodded. They joined Erin at the front door of the high school and Sawyer watched Erin shift into her stern-older-sister mode. The awesome sight made him smile.

Erin tried to wait out Sawyer, hoping he'd talk about what he'd said to Tate on their drive back to town, but her anxiety won out. "So what did my brother say about why he skipped?"

"We didn't talk about it."

"What? Why not?"

"It's obvious you're not a boy."

She frowned. "What's that supposed to mean?"

He held up his hand. "What it means is you don't understand how a teenage boy's mind works. Pushing him would've just made him clam up. I'd be challenging his manhood. He needs some space, then when he feels safe enough or trusts enough, he'll open up."

As much as she didn't want to acknowledge it, his words made sense. "I'm worried that Tate is hurting and doesn't have any way to vent his feelings."

"Is there an adult male he could talk to? Maybe your pastor?"

"Tate's mad, and I think the last person he wants to talk to is our pastor."

"Anyone else?"

"Maybe Auntie's husband, Nelson, but he's not here and he doesn't want to leave his hometown in Bluewater to come and visit us. The last time Uncle left his hometown, it was to go to Vietnam."

"That would do it. Well, Tate invited me out to your ranch to ride, and I might—"

"He did what?" Her voice rose.

"I asked your brother if he knew where I could rent a horse to ride. He told me to come out to the ranch and ride your father's mount."

She felt her jaw drop.

"I told you I was a cowboy, and riding clears my head. Of course, I didn't bring my horse with me, so I'd have to rent a mount. He told me to come to the ranch and ride your dad's horse to exercise him."

Conflicting emotions raced through Erin. If Tate had invited Sawyer to the ranch, maybe her brother might feel free enough to talk to him. "No, no, I wasn't talking about your horse. I'm surprised my brother invited you to come and ride."

Shrugging, he said, "Hey, I'm a likable guy."

His comment didn't deserve an answer, but Sawyer might have hit on a plan. "So, if you come out to the ranch, Tate might want to talk to you."

"Could be. If I come out and ride, and if Tate wants to talk, I'm willing to be a sounding board for him."

"Good. He definitely doesn't want to talk to me."

"That's because you're a girl and his sister. It's easier to talk to a stranger who is not emotionally involved."

He was right. She'd prayed that God would send help for her brother. "Thank you."

She'd just relaxed when Sawyer said, "I also asked your brother about you."

"Why?" She strangled on the word.

Sawyer looked out the passenger-side window, not in any hurry to answer. "I asked how reliable you are."

Curiosity raced through her. "What did Tate say?"

"He said I could count on you. If you were assigned a job, then I didn't need to worry. He laughed and said you had a walking-in-the-clouds mode and sometimes let the little details escape."

Erin's cheeks heated.

Leaning against the door, he studied her.

"I'll admit, when I get focused on something, I commit myself to the project and everything else falls away."

"He's proud of you. And he knows he can count on you."

Her eyes watered and her heart eased. "Thanks for talking with him. And for reminding me he needed my understanding, not my rebuke."

He nodded. "It wasn't brilliant insight, just experience."

Sawyer's words piqued her curiosity, but there was a look in his eyes that stopped her from asking about his personal life.

"Still, I appreciate it."

"No problem. I'm just passing along the encouragement my brother and I have received."

Again, he'd dropped another nugget from his past. "Care to explain?"

He smiled. "That belongs for another time."

She knew he'd slammed the door on his personal life, holding back, but for the first time she wanted to let her heart have free rein to get to know the man who made her smile and her heart sing.

Chapter Five

The rumble of Erin's stomach echoed through the cab of the truck.

Sawyer met her gaze and grinned.

Looking down at his watch, he said, "It's close to two and my stomach agrees with yours. Want to get something to eat?"

She hesitated.

"Skipping lunch isn't going to make anything better. Besides, you might have a different outlook on the situation if you're full," he added.

"Didn't you use that ploy before?"

"It works. And it's true."

She glanced at him and considered his words.

"So, do you want to stop, or do you need to be somewhere else?" he pressed.

"My life's here until Dad gets well, Tate's situation settles down and the rodeo gets on track."

"It sounds like you and I are free and hungry, so let's go eat."

"Do you always ooze charm, or are you just that hungry?"

"Hey, I'm a turnaround specialist, and my job is to bring people together and get cooperation. When people are fed, they're much nicer."

"I know when I'm being handled, but I'm hungry."

When they arrived in town, Erin drove to Lulu's. The lunch crowd had already cleared, so there was no line. Once inside, Sawyer motioned for Erin to order first.

"Good to see you," Lulu said. "I attended the rodeo meeting last week and listened to Sawyer's plan. 'Course, things got a little rowdy toward the end. I liked how Erin settled things down."

"I did, too," Sawyer said.

Pleasure at his words washed through Erin. She felt as if she was fifteen and just discovering boys.

"And when word got out that local people could bid for a job working on the rodeo, that started everyone talking. It's been a long time since this much excitement has rolled through town. Why, my brother, Tom, is going to submit a bid to work on the redo of the iron works for the chutes out on the rodeo ground. I haven't seen him with that much bounce in his step in a long time. Thanks, Sawyer."

"I can't take credit for that. Erin suggested it.

Well, I'd say she vigorously encouraged me to use local residents."

Lulu smiled. "That's our Erin."

"More than one person's told me that."

"It only made sense to use local talent so we can keep money here," Erin added.

"Well, we can use the work," Lulu answered. "So, what do you want for lunch?"

They ordered lunch and settled in a booth.

Erin sat across from him, and he studied her. She searched for something to say. He certainly held his cards close to his vest. He was a man who could be both charming and courageous, but kept his heart shielded. "Thanks for the help with Tate."

"Not a problem."

The tone of his voice didn't invite more conversation. Although she wanted to know more of what her brother had said, she respected that Sawyer wouldn't tell her what they'd talked about.

As he continued to observe her, she wanted to squirm under his scrutiny. Before she could say anything stupid, Rose delivered their burgers.

She vibrated with excitement. "Everyone's talking about the list you put up at Bob's place last week. Jobs. It sounds great. Where do Mom and I sign up for a concession booth? I know people in Harding County want to get in there, and I'm afraid there will be more people who want booths than we have."

"Ask the guy in charge." Erin pointed to Sawyer.

"Electricity, plumbing and sewage have to be addressed," he warned. "Can you and your mother do that?"

Rose gave him a "duh" look. "We do our own work here and do it better than most men."

Erin's eyes danced with amusement.

"I'm surprised, but I admire you."

"Hey, don't underestimate us country girls," Rose informed him.

"I'm quickly learning that lesson."

Sawyer had to remind himself these women in no way resembled his mom or ex-girlfriend. When he turned back to Erin, her eyes danced, and her lips turned up. It was good to see the lightness in her face.

"Okay, you're right."

"Glad you're getting the message."

He grunted and they dug into their hamburgers.

"I'm pleased that the people in this county are eager to help with the rodeo."

"It's a big part of our lives. And the folks who don't ranch have work keeping us ranchers supplied. Rodeo is our time to shine and brag. If you won bareback riding one year, you were the champ all year."

"And you won the barrel racing."

"I did." Pride shone in her eyes. "I had a couple of close calls when I was in high school, but I won. Those were the years I was the proudest." She nodded to the picture on the restaurant wall. "You asked about that picture before. That's one of those years."

He understood. It was a success that others in the community looked up to. Of course, once Caleb and Sawyer had settled in Plainview, his friends found other things besides his rodeo wins that they could admire him for, and they forgot about the two high school orphans living in the back room of the church. Glancing at Erin, he knew she understood.

"I'll contact Norman Burke this afternoon to put out the notice for local bids in his county. I wouldn't want them to say we neglected them."

Erin didn't respond. Looking into her face, he could see her preoccupation. Finally, she snapped out of her thoughts.

"Did you say something?"

"Harding County bids."

"Of course. I'm a little distracted right now. You were going to talk to Norm."

"You heard?"

The door opened and Mel walked in. Erin looked over her shoulder.

Mel's brows plunged into a deep V, making him look like a charging bull. He walked to the table and glared at Erin. She didn't squirm or shrink under his stare.

"Mel, what's wrong?" Sawyer leaned forward.

The man looked ready to explode. "The company that did work on the rodeo the last time called me this morning, and their president told me you wanted him to bid along with everyone else." Everyone in the café heard.

"That's true. What's the problem with that? All companies working on the rodeo reconstruction need to submit a bid. Those bids will be open for anyone to review."

Color flooded Mel's cheeks. He nodded to Erin. "She put you up to that?"

"No," Sawyer replied. "That's standard procedure taught in college. Since the counties are involved with this project, things have to be open to the public."

Mel raised his chin. "I wouldn't be taking advice from her." Mel pointed to Erin. "On our final vote to award the contract, her father voted for you over her, so that should tell you something about her skills." His gaze bored into Erin's. She withstood Mel's caustic words and didn't flinch. "We voted your plan, not hers."

Sawyer felt a flash of anger shoot through him and rose to his feet. Mel knew part of his plan was having everyone submit bids. It was the same in Erin's. Why suddenly was he complaining? What was going on? "I'm proceeding according to my plan, which the board voted on. Erin's answered my questions and filled me in on local resources.

What I'm missing is last year's budget with the final figures that I asked for earlier. Did you leave it in the office for me to review?"

Mel rocked back and forth on his feet as if he readied himself to charge Sawyer.

Sawyer widened his stance and prepared for Mel's actions.

After studying Sawyer, Mel said, "I'll drop it by this afternoon." He turned and stomped out of the building.

Lulu raced out of the kitchen and hugged Erin. "Don't pay attention to that bitter old man. What's wrong with him? Pastor Tony, Father Jones, or Mel's pastor needs to get a hold of the man and do some talking."

Rose planted her hands on her hips. "Or someone needs to talk to Mel's wife. Sharon wouldn't allow such behavior."

Sawyer watched as Erin talked with the other people in the dining room about Mel's cruel behavior.

"I don't know what's gotten into that man," Rose muttered. "I've never seen him so mean. I think I'd rather deal with a rattler than Mel right now."

The other patrons in the café agreed.

Erin grabbed her purse. She looked brittle, as if she were encased in ice. If another person talked to her, it seemed she might shatter. "You want a ride over to the office?" she asked him.

"No, I'll walk."

She nodded.

Sawyer opened the door and allowed her to exit before him. "If I have more questions, I can call you?"

"Of course."

Sawyer walked, mulling over the fact that Erin had taken several blows today and she still stood strong. He found himself admiring her. No, it was more than that. She didn't crumble at the least opposition, and she could be depended on.

And she was beautiful.

Smart.

And he'd be leaving when this job was done.

But a feeling inside him bloomed, no matter how hard his head argued against it.

Erin's mind went blank as she drove home. Everything seemed to have blown up at the same time—her father's stroke, losing the bid for the rodeo job and her brother ditching school. She could've dealt with all that, but the crushing blow that Mel delivered at Lulu's in front of her neighbors and friends—that her father voted for Sawyer over her—had brought her to her knees.

What's going on? Lord, I don't understand.

When had her father stopped believing in her? And she couldn't even ask him now since he hadn't remembered anything of the day of the stroke. Erin hadn't seen much of her mother since she'd decided to stay in Albuquerque to be close to her husband. Had Mother known about her father's vote? When Erin had seen her mother in the hospital, all that had concerned them was Dad's condition. He was alive, but no one knew what had been affected—memory, speech, motor function—but Erin hung on to the hope that her father would completely recover. Anything else, she didn't want to consider.

Mel had delighted in giving her the crushing news in front of a live audience at Lulu's. He could've lied, she told herself, but his claims were easily verified. What had she ever done to Mel to make him hold such contempt for her?

Traci. Erin knew in her bones her old friend feared Erin would try to steal away Andy if she got the job, which was ridiculous. Mel worried about it, too. By the time Erin got home, the entire town would know what had happened at Lulu's. Probably by tonight everyone in Harding and Quay counties would know, too.

Erin pulled into the driveway of the ranch. Tate wasn't back from school yet, so Erin could have a good pity party before she had to act as if everything was normal.

The instant Erin walked into the kitchen and looked at her aunt, Betty asked, "How did things go with Tate?"

"As well as could be expected. The sheriff told Tate he'd have to remove those noisy chrome exhaust pipes or only drive his truck at the dirt track. And he recommended taking away his truck for a while."

"Do you trust him to come home after all the trouble?"

Her heart jerked. "Yes. I think it's his cry to be heard. I pray I'm right." And if she wasn't… she didn't want to consider it.

Betty rose and walked to where Erin stood and enveloped her in a hug. Erin relaxed in Betty's arms. Erin didn't cry but let her aunt's love encircle her.

"Thank you," Erin whispered several minutes later.

Betty pulled back. "I called your mother and we talked. She wants to talk to you tonight. We'll have to drive him to and from school the rest of this week and probably next. He refused to answer why he ditched."

"Tate doesn't want to talk to his sister about what's in his heart."

Betty motioned for Erin to sit, then poured them coffee.

"That's normal. Men are hardheads, and a boy your brother's age doesn't know what to do with his heart."

"Could Uncle talk to him?" Erin asked, hoping.

"Of course, but we'd have to ship him to Bluewater, and Tate would know it was about his behavior, so would he talk?" Betty sighed and studied Erin. "Is there more that's bothering you?"

How her aunt sensed things, Erin would never know. "Sawyer helped me when the sheriff called that he'd picked up Tate. Sawyer rode with Tate back to school, so maybe he could help."

Betty studied her. "That's possible, but what are you holding back?"

Gritting her teeth, Erin didn't want to discuss what had been revealed.

Reaching out, Betty cupped Erin's cheek. "I've diapered you, cared for you as if you were the daughter of my body. Whatever you say will stay with me."

"Father voted for Sawyer to win the rodeo contract over me."

Betty's mouth puckered into an O. "Surely, you are mistaken."

She shook her head. "Mel happily told me while I was at Lulu's and announced it to everyone in the place. He's afraid that I'll influence Sawyer to do things my way. His argument was that if my father didn't believe in me, then Sawyer shouldn't, either."

Betty put her hands over Erin's and squeezed. "Something's not right here. You are the joy of your parents, and I've never heard your father say anything against you. You are his sunflower."

Erin tried to smile. "In his condition, I can't

ask him why. I know it's small of me to question his decision, but—"

"It all seems so dark now, but believe, Daughter. Sometimes God takes us on a journey to let us see a different view. You will have to walk in faith."

The words washed over Erin like a gentle breeze. All she could remember was her father cheering her on when she rode barrels competitively, or his sitting in the front row, beaming with pride when she graduated from high school as the valedictorian.

Her entire life her father had supported her but, over the past few months, she'd noticed a change in him, a hesitancy that put her on alert.

"Thanks, Auntie."

They hugged, and Erin walked into her father's study, ready to search for the final addendum to last year's budget. But, as she surveyed his things, her heart ached with questions and doubt.

Sawyer walked into the rodeo office. The scene at the café had disturbed him. Why had Mel decided to humiliate Erin in front of everyone? The woman had held up under the man's ugly attack, but those small-town currents swirled around them.

When he entered the office, Lisa looked up. She nodded to the meeting room. "Mel brought the budget for the last year."

He nodded.

"Is everything okay?" Lisa asked.

"Mel seems on some sort of mission to hurt Erin."

"I heard."

The speed with which the news spread in a small town amazed Sawyer. None of the major cell phone carriers could've acted quicker.

"Could you explain the situation to me? I want to know when to duck." He moved toward her desk and collapsed in the chair beside her.

Lisa explained the complicated history of the two women and the one guy.

"But if Traci's happily married, why would Mel be so hard on Erin? She's been gone at school and riding the rodeo circuit."

Lisa leaned closer to Sawyer. "When the board decided to redo the facilities, Erin put in her bid. I think Traci's worried that if Erin's in town for that long maybe the feelings Andy had for Erin might flare back to life."

"That's ridiculous." Sawyer ran his fingers through his hair. "How long have Traci and Andy been married?"

"Almost nine years, but folks have noticed things are a little strained between the two."

A frown knit his brow. "You're telling me Mel's worried about the situation?"

"You asked what the problem was." Lisa

shrugged. "It might not make sense, but there it is."

What a mess. "Thanks for the heads-up." Now at least he knew where the potholes were. Maybe he could survive this job. But he doubted he'd ever be the same.

Chapter Six

Late the next afternoon, Sawyer drove back from his successful meeting with the Harding County members of the rodeo board. They'd been excited about having their residents bid for contracts to do work for the rodeo. Norman had last year's budget and let Sawyer take the notebook to compare with the ones Mel brought to the office.

During the meeting, thoughts of Erin kept creeping into Sawyer's head while he talked to Norman. What had gotten into him?

When he passed the road leading to the Delong ranch, Sawyer went with his gut and decided to visit Erin. He'd go with the nagging feeling that he'd experienced all afternoon. Besides, he could use the excuse that he wanted to ride. He was a cowboy.

He parked his truck and saw Erin in the corral beyond, practicing her barrel racing. He sat for a moment and watched her ride the figure eights. Slipping out of his truck, he softly closed the door.

She didn't bounce in her saddle or yank on the reins. She leaned into the sharp turn, pushing down in the stirrups, keeping her weight off the horse's back. They worked in unison as a well-oiled machine. When she finished the last figure eight, she let her horse canter around the corral, cooling both her and the horse.

"You've got a good seat."

"Hours of practice."

Her face glowed, and her entire body appeared relaxed and at ease, the most relaxed he'd ever seen her. This was a joyful woman, who loved riding and competing. As she came toward him, he felt himself being drawn to that smile. Her bay-colored mare had a black mane and black points.

"Nice mount."

"Wind Dancer is a spoiled girl, but she loves to compete. The only thing she wants to do more than compete is to ride across our ranch."

Sawyer laid his palm on the horse's light reddish coat and stroked her.

Erin patted the horse's neck. "I needed to ride her again. We were competing in Denver when I got news of Dad's stroke. I drove home, left her here and then went on to Albuquerque. Both Dancer and I need the routine of doing the barrels. It's a comfort. She's a bit of a high-maintenance girl. You should understand."

"I do. Fortunately, my brother promised to keep my horse, Rescue, in shape.

"Thinking about it, I remembered more of you and your brother at the charity rodeo. You were quite a team doing pickup."

"Thanks. I was a little rusty at that affair, but Caleb wanted the backup. Pickup is Caleb's specialty, and when he practiced, I worked with him, so I've done it before."

"So why didn't you bring your horse with you here?"

"For a while, I traveled with Rescue, but he got tired of moving around, so I left him with my brother. When I was driving by your ranch, the urge hit me, and since Tate said I could ride anytime I wanted, I thought I'd go with the flow." He leaned against the fence post. "I'm sure Tate didn't think I'd take up his offer so quickly, but… Besides, Tate mentioned your dad's horse might need to be exercised, so on the drive back from Harding County, I thought about it. He'll probably be surprised to find me here."

"He's not home, yet. This is the first day we've driven him to school, and he wasn't too happy with me this morning. Betty took the evening shift." She dismounted, patted Dancer and looked at her watch. "Besides, having to endure his scowls and glares can only be tolerated once a day. He'll be glad for an excuse to get away from us. You're welcome to wait for him."

"I'll do that. Thanks."

After unsaddling Dancer, Erin walked the horse to the corral and let her loose.

Sawyer joined her at the fence. "Today, I drove to Harding County and talked to those board members about opening for bids," he said, leaning against the fence.

"Why not just call?"

"I did yesterday, but I wanted to see the county, meet face-to-face with people. They liked the suggestion of locals getting involved in the revitalization."

He caught her smile.

"It's good to see everyone get involved. The more the project is talked up and the word spread, the more support you'll have. Excitement will build and you'll get free publicity."

Erin didn't look at him, but kept her gaze on Dancer.

Sawyer wanted to say something to her about what had happened at Lulu's yesterday, or what he learned from Lisa, but if she didn't mention it, then he wouldn't. She seemed to be doing well today.

"I did get Norman's copy of the rodeo financials for the last year. Since he's the top board member in Harding it will be interesting to see how it compares with the book Mel dropped off after lunch yesterday and the one I've looked at here."

Erin turned to him. "Mel brought the notebook by yesterday?"

Sawyer carefully searched her eyes. "Yes, and I glanced at it last night, but I didn't see any final numbers." He shrugged. "I wanted to see if Norman and Mel even have the same estimates."

The sound of a car in the drive drew their attention. Moments later, the doors slammed and Tate appeared. He took in the situation. Betty was slow getting out of the truck.

Sawyer stepped away from the fence. "I had an urge to ride this afternoon." He knew that both Erin and her brother would understand. They were all horse people.

Tate rubbed his neck. "Ridin' sounds good to me, and since I'm being supervised, you can't object." Tate aimed his comment at his sister.

Sawyer inwardly cringed. Tate's heavy-handed approach invited trouble. "Since I don't know your ranch, a guide would be a good idea, if that's okay with you, Erin. If something happened to me while riding here—" he shrugged "—people might think it was your way of getting rid of the competition." He grinned, hoping his light tone would ease the tension between brother and sister.

She caught the teasing mood. "Well, you've got a point. I wouldn't want to be accused of letting our new rodeo wrangler get lost."

"No one would accuse you of ignoring your duty," Tate snapped.

Her brother's irritation at being driven to and from school was showing.

"Well, it's a good idea for you to accompany Sawyer."

Tate started toward the other horses.

"Just know, brother," Erin called, "we'll have a talk later about school today."

Tate froze. "Okay."

As they walked away, Sawyer gave her a nod of approval.

Erin smiled.

"When I drove up today, your sister was practicing her barrels," Sawyer told Tate as they rode past the practice corral. Sawyer wanted to get Tate's mind off school.

After several moments of silence, Tate replied, "She always practices. Both Sis and Dancer love it. Sis took Dancer with her to the university. I don't know how she practiced, but she did. I understood her wanting to ride, but others didn't." Tate's shoulders straightened with the pride that rang in his voice.

"I did the same and took my horse, Rescue, with me to school and rode on the weekends. You can relax and let problems melt away on the back of a horse. Life seems to come into focus." And no better place to pray than on the back of his horse. "It was only after I graduated and took jobs in different cities that I left Rescue at my brother's ranch. I do miss Rescue. When I call my brother, I ask about my horse before his wife."

"Really? You should use FaceTime to talk to your horse. It's what Sis uses every night to talk to Mom about Dad's condition."

"That's a good idea. I think I might try that the next time. Question is, will my brother take the tablet into the barn? But that won't replace riding my horse."

"True. Sometimes things aren't the way you want them." The comment trailed off.

There it was. Tate's cry for help.

"Yes, but things happen that we don't have a say in. When my dad had a heart attack, he didn't survive."

Tate remained quiet.

"So what'd you do?" he finally asked.

"There's nothing you can do but survive. I had my big brother and we got through it together. Got closer." Sawyer wouldn't tell Tate the other ugly part of his story. Tate needed to be encouraged, not depressed. "Your dad survived the stroke."

"But nothing's going to be the same. I should've been better and spent time with him."

Lord, help. "We can't go back and change the past, but going forward you can. You can be there for your dad in the future. And I know your sister is also struggling with your dad's stroke and with me winning the bid. I think you could help her."

"She's strong."

"True, but is there anyone there for her? We all need others to help us. I think she might like someone she could depend on to be there for her." Sawyer guided his mount down a wash.

Tate eyed him. "Really?"

"Yup. I knew this sheriff who had a reputation of being the best and, in his state, everyone depended on him, but when he went home, his wife made all the decisions in the house. The sheriff just needed a moment to be taken care of, but when he went to work, he was in charge.

"I couldn't change my dad dying. It took me a long time, and a lot of anger, to accept. But there was a pastor who showed an angry boy that he needed to let God into his heart and do the work." It still awed Sawyer how patiently and gently the pastor had guided two young wounded men.

Tate eyed him, then looked back at the landscape, his shoulders tense.

At least Sawyer had put the ideas into the teen's head. "I think we need to start back. We don't want to worry anyone."

Turning toward the ranch, an easy silence settled between them.

The first hurdle with Tate had been cleared.

* * *

They could see the ranch house on the horizon when they heard the ring of a meal triangle.

"We're being called to dinner," Tate said. "I'm hungry."

"You're a teenager and that's to be expected." They traded grins.

"We need to hurry back, and I should get going back to town."

"Why don't you stay and eat with us?"

"I'm sure your aunt isn't expecting me."

"Didn't you listen last Sunday? My aunt loves feeding others. It's her thing. No one is ever turned away. In fact, she'll tackle you before you can come up with an excuse to leave."

Sawyer laughed. "Another determined woman."

Tate shook his head. "Us guys don't stand a chance between my mom, Auntie, and sister."

"Well, consider me on your side."

They rode up to the barn, unsaddled their mounts and put them in the corral.

Before Sawyer could walk out of the corral, Betty appeared on the porch and waved them inside. "I'm ready to put dinner on the table. Hustle."

"I told you," Tate whispered.

Sawyer didn't want to impose but thought he needed to excuse himself before he left to go back into town, eat and go over the information he collected in Mosquero, the county seat of Harding County.

Ten minutes later, Sawyer knew it was impossible to endure a tornado and remain standing.

As he sat next to Tate at the table, the teen couldn't help but smile.

Betty put the main dish on the table. "Erin, where are you?"

She raced into the room. "I'm sorry, Auntie. I was looking through some of Dad's notebooks concerning the rodeo."

Erin settled across the table from Tate and Sawyer.

After saying grace, Betty started passing dishes. She handed Tate a bowl of greens to go with his roasted chicken. "How was your day, Tate?"

Everyone froze.

Tate refused to look at Betty. They hadn't talked about Tate's little stunt yesterday. Erin had told her brother they would wait a day to cool down and think about what happened. The only thing they'd determined was that Tate wouldn't be driving.

"I talked to your mother this morning. She asked about you," Betty said.

Sawyer leaned close and whispered, "I think she knows."

Tate's lips tightened.

"What were you thinking?" Betty asked.

"Auntie," Erin answered. "I think we've all been stressed with what's happened. It doesn't excuse it, but explains it." She met her brother's surprised look.

"True," Betty replied, "but remember what your mother and grandmother said—you do wrong, you pay the price. When all five of us kids were growing up, Grandma wasn't interested in excuses. Later, after we paid the price, paid the penalty, Grandma would sit with whatever child had done wrong, talk about what had happened and ask if we had learned a lesson. Or, she would have us think of a better way to have handled things."

"Tate and I were going to talk about it after dinner," Erin said.

Waving her hand, Betty said, "Now's a good time."

"I don't think Tate would want us to discuss the topic here over dinner."

"What Tate needs to know is that he's responsible for his actions," Betty replied.

"I know I'm stepping into an argument where I don't have a vote in the outcome, but I think Tate knows he's made a mistake." Sawyer glanced at Tate for permission to argue for him. The teen nodded.

Sawyer continued. "We talked on our ride. And

I think he's willing to pay whatever price you think is appropriate."

Silence settled on the room.

Erin folded her hands on the table. "Mom and I talked. She thinks that what we've done so far, Tate not driving this next week but having either me or Auntie drive him, is a good start."

Tate opened his mouth to protest.

"How long?" Sawyer asked, jumping in.

"A week at least," Erin replied, "or until Tate builds our trust in him, again."

Sawyer turned to Tate. "I think that's reasonable, don't you?" To simply take away Tate's truck sounded like a reprieve to Sawyer, and he hoped the boy realized his mother had gone easy on him.

Tate didn't immediately answer. He slowly surveyed each person at the table. Heaving a sigh, Tate nodded. "Okay."

"Mom said that your truck needs to stay in the driveway. She'll take up the issue of the tailpipes with you when she comes home. It doesn't make a difference if you are a senior—ditching will not be accepted. There is a price to pay."

Tate's mouth tightened. "Does she want my keys?"

"No. She's going to trust you and give you the opportunity to show we can trust your word. What happens now is on your shoulders."

"I get it."

"Well, with all that taken care of, let's clear the dishes and Tate can finish his homework," Betty said.

Erin breathed a sigh of relief. The ride with Sawyer seemed to have helped her brother's attitude. She'd intended to talk privately to Tate and prayed Betty forcing the issue wouldn't backfire and, amazingly, it hadn't.

Erin owed Sawyer a debt.

"Thanks for helping with Tate."

"Not a problem."

"You mentioned you have Norman's books with you. Would you mind if I looked through that set, too, to compare with Dad's?"

Sawyer set the last dish on the counter. "No, I don't mind."

Betty waved them out of the kitchen. "Go, talk."

"I'll get them."

Sawyer disappeared out the back door and showed up in the library minutes later.

"I wonder if the figures in Norman's budgets are the final ones, because we haven't located a set yet."

"I hope so, too. I haven't been able to study Mel's numbers thoroughly yet, since we've been swamped with inquiries about jobs at the office, with people wanting to submit bids." He sat beside Erin on the small couch in the office so they could look at the figures together.

Opening Norman's budget to compare with her dad's, they had to dodge the front covers to avoid being smacked. With their dance, Erin and Sawyer bumped into each other, laughing and grinning like children. Suddenly, she felt Sawyer's warmth up and down her right side like the heat of a campfire. She froze. So did he.

Trying to ignore his presence, she compared the first pages of the budgets, but her stomach felt as if she had swallowed jumping beans. Turning her head, she came face-to-face with Sawyer. Inches separated them. She could see the green-and-brown color of his hazel eyes. A brown dot sat outside the pupil in the iris of his right eye.

They could hear the ticking of the grandfather clock in the study. She wondered if he could hear the pounding of her heart.

"These aren't final numbers, either. These are the same as the ones in the other notebooks."

His gaze held hers hostage, then he smiled, a soft, welcoming, toe-curling smile. "I'll compare all three notebooks when I get back."

Erin pulled the sticky note she found and showed it to Sawyer. "This is the note I told you about. Apparently, Mel told dad he'd get them the final numbers, but so far, we haven't seen them."

"And it seems no one has seen those numbers."

"So why are they missing?" Erin asked.

"That's the burning question we all want answered."

She closed the binder and held onto the edges. "It seems you keep coming to Tate's rescue."

"Well, I just wanted to help the kid along. I had my fair share of troubles as a teen."

"I wasn't criticizing, but thanking you."

He shrugged. "I know what it's like having your world turned upside down and not knowing how to act. I want to help."

She wanted more, wanted to know how his life had been turned upside down, but again he held back, not filling in the blanks. It seemed so unfair that their lives were open books but Sawyer volunteered nothing of himself.

Covering her hand with his, he lightly squeezed. She didn't look up at him. "When you don't know what to say, it helps when someone else steps in. And there's been so much going on I wasn't as careful about Tate's needs." She stared at their intertwined hands and pulled away. "I don't think anyone was. With the rest of the people in the household women, Dad made sure Tate knew it was the boys against the girls. I guess Tate felt his only support was gone."

"Realize boys don't respond to 'Let's talk.' You could invite him to go riding or help him clean out the stalls, then you can try talking to him."

"That makes sense. Tate and Dad spent lots of

time out on the range or in the barn. Sometimes, they liked to take their fishing poles and go to the creek and fish. That's a sport I don't understand, sitting there waiting on a fish."

"Spoken like a woman who doesn't understand the finer points of fishing."

She really should stand. Maybe then she wouldn't be so rattled, but her body refused to cooperate.

"Did any of the rodeo events appeal to your brother?"

She gathered her scattered thoughts. "He did 4-H projects. He won for raising the best heifer in the state when he was in the ninth grade. He earned a lot of money, but that didn't stop several of the boys at school from teasing him about just winning for raising a cow. They asked why he didn't compete in real rodeo stuff like bull ridin' or bareback ridin'. Dad told him—" Her voice trailed off. Suddenly, the light shone in her brain. Her gaze collided with his and she saw an understanding, and humor.

"Dad always did things with Tate and then talked with him. Ah, I see what you're saying. You have to *be* with them, doing their favorite activity before you can talk, unlike us women who can sit down and discuss things."

"I never doubted it."

Looking down at her hands, she shook her head. "Mom and Auntie tell me I should walk softly sometimes and see what's around me. See the path God has sent me down."

Leaning closer, he whispered, "I'd listen to them."

The door to the study opened, making Sawyer sit up straight. Betty leaned into the room.

"Your mother is on the phone."

Erin hadn't heard the ringing.

"She wants to talk to you. She's speaking to Tate now."

Erin and Sawyer stood.

"I need to get going." He grabbed the notebook he'd brought in and her father's. "I'll compare these with the ones Mel left, if that's all right with you."

She nodded and followed him out to his truck.

Betty and Erin followed. They stopped at the screen door and watched as his taillights disappeared around the curve of the road.

Betty wrapped her arm around Erin's shoulder and squeezed. "I think I know why that man got the contract."

"Why?" What was her aunt talking about?

Betty dropped her arm and turned to face Erin. "God sends us those people we need on our journey, and perhaps this family needed Sawyer to help us through this difficult time." Betty didn't wait for a response but continued. "Heaven knew your brother would have problems that neither of us could imagine, and He sent Sawyer. You must admit that Tate's experienced some bad spots that neither you nor I thought about. I know your mother wanted me here just as a touchstone and someone to feed you and Tate."

Erin couldn't believe her ears. "Really, Auntie? I was to lose so Sawyer could be here to help Tate?"

"I can see that. Remember, God knows the end of the story."

Erin frowned at Betty, confounded by her words.

"I can see you don't understand me. Open your heart and listen to God."

Auntie did have an uncanny way of knowing things, but this time she'd completely missed the mark. Completely. Sawyer wasn't here to minister to her family.

So did she have a better explanation?

No, but it wasn't to help the Delong family, that much she knew.

But her heart called her out, saying she refused to face the truth.

Chapter Seven

Sawyer returned to the rodeo office. When he opened the front door, he stood for a moment, listening to the silence. He flipped on the lights and went to the meeting room. He could've waited until tomorrow to compare Norman's and Detrick's notebooks to the ones in the office, but he wanted to resolve the nagging question tonight.

He put the binders on the table beside the one Mel had left yesterday and compared the three. They all were the same, but none of them had final numbers.

Leaning back in his seat, he thought about the situation. The nagging feeling that something was wrong didn't go away. Instead, it got stronger. Why?

"What are you doing here at this hour?" Traci stood in the doorway of the boardroom.

"Working."

She slowly walked to the table, eyeing the notebooks. "It's after dinner and you should be in your hotel room, relaxing."

He swallowed his irritation. "I'm sure the rodeo board wouldn't object. I think they'd want the most for their money."

"Could be." She walked around the room.

Her sudden appearance made him suspicious. "What are you doing here?"

"I saw the light when I drove by and wanted to know who was here this late. I thought Dad might be here, and I wanted to talk to him." She studied the binders. "Why do you need last year's budget?" Her voice hardened. "And why three copies? I don't understand."

How could he get out of this mess? "I wanted to look at last year's budget to compare costs, and I couldn't find it. I asked the secretary where it was since it wasn't with the others. Oddly, her copies, hard and electronic, were missing, too. When your dad stopped by the office before he left town, I asked him where it was. Then, today, I got one from Norman when I was in Harding County. On the way home, I stopped by the De-long ranch to ride with Tate, and Erin gave me her father's copy."

Her eyes narrowed. "Aren't you showing a little too much partiality, stopping by Erin's?"

The tone of her voice made the hairs on the back of his neck stand up. He didn't like what she implied, but he needed to tread carefully in this situation. "Tate offered the opportunity to ride and, after driving all day, when I went by the Delong ranch, I knew I needed to unwind on the back of a horse. Ever have one of those days?"

Traci's frown eased.

"Yes, I have."

He picked up the notebooks. "It's been a long day, and I'm ready to call it quits." He motioned for her to exit the room before him, and he turned off the lights, then locked the office.

Traci tapped her lips with her index finger. "I have an idea. Why don't I document the rodeo redo with pictures? I could do a website and everyone in Harding and Quay counties will know the progress of things. And, if we need more people to bid on jobs that come up, we could put the notice there."

Traci had struck gold.

"I've already listed some of the job openings on the website, but I like your idea. You could do a new website and add a link to it or just rework the current site." The more Sawyer thought about it, the more he liked it.

"I can do it. I'm sure my dad would want me doing that."

A website would keep everyone informed and would keep Traci busy. He sensed that if she had a purpose, other problems might be avoided. "Go for it."

She smiled, leaned over and kissed his cheek. "Thanks. I'll work on it tonight."

Sawyer sat down on the bed, then pulled off his boots. What a couple of days. He should've been exhausted, but each time he closed his eyes, a different scene popped into his brain, from taking Tate home, to Mel gladly telling Erin her father had voted for him, to the trip to the next county with all those eager faces who wanted to bid on rodeo jobs.

He didn't know what Traci had planned to do when she'd shown up at the office, but it didn't matter, because her idea of documenting the redo on the website was a winner. He could see that as the best way to keep people updated and have all the contracts out there for everyone to see. He'd learned that secrets created gossip and gossip developed into grumbling, and he couldn't afford that in a small town.

Stretching out on the bed, he thought about the afternoon ride with Tate. Sawyer had read the situation correctly. The youth needed someone to talk to. Sawyer thought of Pastor Garvey, who had guided him. The man had shepherded both Sawyer and his brother, showing them what normal family life was. Garvey had stood in the gap, being there for them. Sawyer wanted to pass on that comfort he had received from the pastor.

He sat up and looked through the notebooks

he'd brought back to the room with him. In the middle of reviewing the bid for last year's concrete work, his brain shifted to being stuffed beside Erin on that small sofa. His heart had sped up as if he'd been bull riding. He didn't like going with emotions, but this time had been different.

He had expected resistance from Erin over the rodeo—or some form of sabotage—since this had been his experience with other women in his life. Instead, she had contributed good, constructive ideas. Ideas that made his plan better, which awed him. How different was this experience from all the previous encounters he'd had with other females in his life?

The more he knew of Erin, the more she reminded him of his sister-in-law and not his mother or ex-girlfriend. So how did he deal with that? His mother needed both of her sons' input before she could make a decision. If not them, she sought the approval of her current boyfriend. Erin had her ideas, but she worked with others to accomplish her vision. What a difference. And he found he liked how Erin operated. A lot.

"C'mon, Sawyer, you like more than the way she operates." His words echoed in the room.

When Erin went to the rodeo office the next morning, she noticed Traci's truck sitting in the parking lot. Going into the conference room, Erin saw Traci sitting in front of her laptop. No one else was here. Traci looked up, wariness in her expression.

A dozen different thoughts raced through Erin's head, but what came out of her mouth was, "What are you doing here?" Not elegant, but not hostile.

Traci's jaw flexed. "I'm developing a new website for the rodeo, listing all the jobs that need to be let. I also discussed with Sawyer last night a section of the site where the progress on the current work could be posted."

All of Erin's awkwardness dissolved. "I like that." The words tumbled out of her mouth, but she meant them. "You suggested that?"

Traci nodded and her shoulders relaxed. "I did. It only makes sense in this day and age. There is so much we could do with a website besides posting current job openings—we could show progress on work and collect ideas. The news would be at people's fingertips."

"May I see what you've done so far?" Erin asked.

"Sure."

Erin walked to where Traci sat and looked at the laptop.

"I thought this would let everyone know what the site was for and that it was the new one." A picture of the rodeo grounds was the banner across the top.

"I like that, and those graphics are good.

There's a picture of Jessie Reynolds's winning ride on that bull several years ago that might look good with what you've got there. A collage effect, maybe."

"I hear ya. And there are other pictures we could add."

"True."

Erin sat and ideas started bouncing between them, and the awkwardness of the past few years melted away.

Forty-five minutes later, Sawyer walked into the office. The place hummed with activity.

"Morning, Lisa, what's going on?"

The secretary laughed. "I don't know what you did to Traci, but she's in the boardroom with Erin working."

His heart beating fast, Sawyer raced to the boardroom door, worried about what he'd find. Someone knocked out. Books scattered around. Broken furniture. "Everything okay in here?" He hung on to the door frame.

Erin and Traci looked up.

"Are you always this late?" Traci asked.

"I ate and had coffee," he mumbled, feeling as if he'd run into the door.

"We've been working on the website for the rodeo overhaul for some time," Traci replied.

"If you have suggestions on how we've set it up, or linked the new site to the old, now's the time to put in your two cents' worth," Erin added. "If we officially want to use the new website, then the board will have to approve it, but adding it shouldn't be a problem."

Still dazed, he walked to the table, sat and reviewed what they had done.

"We're almost done, and we're to the point where we need your input on the jobs you want to list and other general information you want given out to the public. Later, I'll take pictures," Traci added.

"Okay." He felt disoriented, as if he'd been plunged into a new reality.

Traci smiled. "Once I got home, all sorts of other ideas popped into my head. We can document the changes, have a blog, open it to suggestions, and everyone can follow the progress and feel involved."

Sawyer shook his head, still unable to believe the change between the women. Was he dreaming?

"I agree," Erin said. "This is a good way to give information out. The more people know, the easier I think it will be. Of course, Sawyer could be the arbiter of the suggestions."

He felt rooted to the floor.

Lisa peeked in and grinned at Sawyer, giving him a thumbs-up, and went back to her desk. Still dazed, he wandered out to the reception area.

"What just happened in there?" he asked, collapsing in the chair by Lisa's desk. "I was prepared to throw my body between the combating opponents. Instead, they've started working together as if they've known each other for ages."

"They have." Lisa's eyes watered up.

"What?" Sawyer panicked.

"It's nice to see those two working together again. Once the initial excitement wears off, there might be some stiffness between them, but at least they're talking." She smiled at him. "Thank you."

Erin appeared at the door to the boardroom. "Sawyer, you need to write up the jobs—and the sooner the better. Traci will have the links to apply for the jobs. Or, if you need me to do that, I will." She disappeared back into the boardroom.

"Did a tornado just run through the building?" he mumbled.

Lisa grinned. "It did, and you're fortunate you're still standing."

The morning turned into a whirlwind of activity with Erin and Traci working together on the website. Sawyer joined the group, writing up the job descriptions. By one o'clock in the afternoon, they had the website up and running. Traci had promised to drive to the rodeo grounds and put the pictures of what needed to be done along with the job descriptions. They retreated to Lulu's for lunch.

Several of the patrons did a double take as if looking at a mirage, with Sawyer, Erin and Traci eating and laughing together.

Bob Rivera walked into the restaurant and froze when he saw the three of them at a table, talking. After a moment, he said, "Am I hallucinating?" He studied each person at the table.

Traci laughed.

"No," Erin answered. "You're awake."

He rubbed his neck. "Then what am I missing?"

"We've decided to set up a new website for the rodeo." Sawyer explained what they had accomplished so far. "It's linked to the old website."

Traci chuckled. Erin couldn't remember the last time she'd seen Traci smile. But this morning, it was like working with an old friend. They had meshed so easily. Erin knew exactly what Traci needed before she opened her mouth.

Bob hadn't moved and kept looking at them. "I'm still not sure this is reality."

Erin waved him in. "Bob, we decided walking down to your store and posting the jobs wasn't the most efficient way to do things. The people in Harding might miss out on opportunities, and this is the best way to get the news out."

"Aren't you worried that some people don't have access to the internet?"

Traci shook her head. "Everyone in either county has a child, grandchild or a neighbor that has access, and those teens are willing to tell their neighbors. Ever try to keep a secret from your teen? If you're worried, we can put the web address at your place."

The lightbulb went off in Bob's head and an 'aha' look crossed his face. "I hear you. I wasn't thinking."

Traci's prediction came true. By the end of the day, everyone in Quay and Harding counties knew about the website. Countless calls and emails had come into the office, which pleased Sawyer. He watched in awe as Erin worked with Traci. The secretary also didn't believe her eyes. She walked countless times into the boardroom and looked. The last time she walked in, Sawyer drew her to the side.

"What's wrong?"

"I keep thinking I'm dreaming and want to pinch myself."

"You're not."

She walked out, shaking her head.

As Traci, Erin and Sawyer left the office at five, Mel walked in. He speared Sawyer with a glare.

"What exactly is going on here?"

Mel's angry demand caught everyone off guard. Sawyer's protective edge roared to life by stepping in front of the women. "We've been working on an interactive website for the rodeo. Traci did the bulk of the work."

The smiles and laughter evaporated.

Sawyer's answer stopped Mel. His gaze shifted from his daughter to Sawyer and, lastly, back to Traci.

"What's wrong, Dad?"

Mel took a deep breath and stepped back. Obviously, he was trying to regroup. "I just drove back from Albuquerque, after talking with the company that does the concrete work for the rodeo. I wanted to see them face-to-face to make sure everything was all right with them. They noted how things had changed." Mel directed his comment to Sawyer.

Erin started to answer, but Sawyer cut her off. "Mel, we discussed this before. Doing it online will speed things up."

Mel's irritation didn't diminish. "I know, but the Johnson Brothers have been working with the rodeo for the last fifteen years and I wanted to explain to them face-to-face how we were doing the bidding now. Since they're the biggest concrete manufacturer in the state, it's assumed they'd get the job. It would've been nice to have a heads-up." He flushed, jutting out his chin.

"I'm sorry, Mel. I thought that's why the board hired me to bring this project in as close to budget as possible, but all jobs need to go through the same process. We want everything we do to be aboveboard, and we want to let everyone see our costs and be able to answer their questions."

Mel's mouth tightened. Sawyer's answer obviously didn't sit well with him, but if he protested further, questions would arise.

He brought his chin down with a firm movement. "Next time, warn me. I just don't want to be hanging out there, looking like an amateur."

"The Johnson Brothers know better, Mel. There's a contract process they go through with government entities," Erin pointed out.

"I know that," he snarled.

Something wasn't right. Sawyer traded glances with Erin and Traci. From their expressions, they thought so, too. Why complain about something the Johnson brothers knew they had to do to get a job?

"Let's go, Traci. Your mom is waiting on us."

Mel and his daughter drove off in different cars. Erin and Sawyer stood there in the quiet night. In the distance, they could hear children playing and an occasional car or truck drive by.

Things were going so well.

"Where's your car?" Erin looked around the parking lot.

"I walked. I like the option of walking on this job." Sawyer stepped closer to Erin. "How's your brother?"

"I haven't gotten a call from the school or my aunt, so I assume everything is good."

"Since you didn't leave when school was over, I assume that Betty picked up Tate."

"Auntie and I agreed she would do afternoon duty if I'd take morning." She opened her truck door. "I don't know who is being punished the most—Tate, Auntie or me."

He walked around the car and stood face-to-face with Erin. "It will be worth the price in the end. You're showing him that he matters."

He wanted to say more than just "hang in there." She cocked her head as if she understood his old hurts. "I'll remember that in the morning when I have to dash to the school at eight fifteen." She opened her car door.

"You surprised me today," Sawyer said, stepping closer.

She stood in the V of the open door. "How's that?"

"When you learned about Traci working on the website, I expected you to object, but you didn't. You sat down and worked with her. Why?"

She hesitated. "Traci won several awards for her website designs. She's good and she has a talent for it, and for me to object didn't make sense."

Lots of people he knew wouldn't have taken that broad view. With every turn of the rodeo redo, this woman surprised him, kept him off guard. She acted with courage and grace, and his admiration for her was growing. No, it was more than admiration, but he wasn't ready to admit what emotion it was.

"Why don't you hop inside and I'll drive you to the hotel? I feel like there's a neon light shining on us for everyone to see." She unlocked his door from the panel on the driver's door.

"Are you going to ask more questions if you drive me to the hotel?" Sawyer asked.

"No, but I might answer some."

He raced around the truck and hopped in. Quiet ruled in the cab on the short drive. She parked in front of his room.

"I'm going to explain some things. Traci's ideas on the website were good, and I asked her about the different ideas she had for the setup. It made sense for her to do it."

"But you and she haven't been getting along," Sawyer commented. He had been talking to people in town. He didn't want to walk into a war zone.

"Traci does excellent work with her websites and graphics. She's set up websites for different people in town and around the county."

He stared at her, as if to make sure she wasn't teasing him. "Why this change?"

"Because, as Traci told me about her ideas, I suddenly realized how much I missed talking to her. How my life had diminished since our… dustup. Fight?"

"Fight? I heard it was more like a major battle."

"It ended our friendship. I really didn't realize the depth of her feelings for Andy. I knew I didn't love Andy enough to marry him. I wanted to go to college, compete on the rodeo circuit and do things I couldn't if I stayed here. I had big dreams, and getting married wasn't one of them." She shook her head. "Looking back on some of the comments Traci made, I can see she had feelings for Andy."

"I heard that blowout wasn't your fault."

"I could've handled things better, but I didn't try." She took a breath and rested her head on the headrest. "As a matter of fact, I think you should let Traci run the website. You could check out bids and then decide which ones are the best."

He considered her idea, but he wasn't that comfortable trusting Traci at this point. "I might ask you if the person doing the bidding is up to the job."

Erin nodded. "Sure, or ask the secretary. You could even check the person out with Lulu."

He noticed her list of who to check with. "Not Mel or Traci?"

"At this point, things are still too new and shaky." She shrugged. "Traci is too involved with her dad. And, lately, Mel's actions are off."

Lencho walked out of the office and he looked into the driver's seat.

Erin rolled down her window and smiled, feeling like a high school girl being caught by her parents out in the car.

"Is everything all right here?" Lencho asked.

"We're talking about the website." Sawyer leaned forward to see the teen's face. "You know that we took it live a few minutes ago."

"You're fooling me," Lencho said.

He gave the address of the domain. "Check it out," Sawyer instructed. "Tell us what you think and look over the jobs that need to be done."

"Lencho, we need you to spread the word about it. It's the future of rodeo, so we want to be cutting-edge," Erin explained.

Leaning down, he addressed Sawyer. "I like the idea. I'll go look." He turned and dashed into the lobby.

"Maybe we won't have to do any advertising."

"You're right."

Sawyer started to lean closer to brush a kiss across her lips. Then they heard a door slam. He jerked up straight and slipped out of the car and walked to his room.

What was happening? Next thing he knew, he'd want to court her. He needed to remember he had a job to do here and nothing else.

Chapter Eight

Erin sat in her dad's office. "Thank You, Lord. Dad's getting better and better." She took a deep, steadying breath. The doctors couldn't say the extent of the damage caused by the stroke. Time would tell. Since her sister was there in the city finishing her degree at the university, Kai would visit the hospital daily, bring her iPad and they'd FaceTime. Erin felt torn between driving to Albuquerque to be with her father and staying put, tending to the rodeo, which she knew he wanted. When she'd suggested coming to see him, both her parents had nixed the idea. They counted on her to oversee the redo.

Where had the week gone? The days melted one into another and there wasn't a moment when they weren't all busy. Lencho had his pulse on the pipeline of information. Within a day, everyone in the county knew about the job openings and every proposal had been bid on.

Sawyer asked about the people who bid on the different jobs and listened to Erin and Traci give him background on them.

Erin savored the process. The man listened to her. He argued his position. Sometimes his ideas were better than hers, and sometimes it went the other way. She loved it and had never felt so alive. She felt herself blooming, growing and being challenged in a way she hadn't before. The unique experience burrowed into her heart, especially after the near miss of a kiss in the library and again last night at his motel. The back door crashed against the wall and it sounded as if a herd of horses were running through the house. Erin stood, hurried to the library door and caught a glimpse of Tate's face, which resembled a thundercloud. He stomped past her and into his room, slamming the door behind him. Amazingly, the door stayed on its hinges. Erin looked back and saw Betty's sober expression. She shook her head.

Erin walked into the kitchen. "What's wrong?"

Betty sighed. "Some boy yelled out that Delong's ride was here. Another boy mentioned that his mama quit picking him up when he was in the first grade. It didn't go well after that." She poured herself a glass of water and sat at the table. "I wanted to get out of the car and straighten that young man out, but I knew it would make things worse for your brother."

Erin wanted to go and talk to him but stopped

herself, knowing that Sawyer would recommend leaving her brother alone for a while.

"You're not going to talk to Tate?"

"No."

Betty studied her. "What happened?"

"Sawyer's made me realize that sometimes, with a young man, you don't have to have the answer immediately. You wait until they are ready."

"Ah, a wise man."

Erin shrugged. "I don't know if I'd call him a wise man, but he is helping me understand things from Tate's view."

"I think Sawyer's thinking is wise."

"I heard my name mentioned," Sawyer called out from the walk leading to the back door. Obviously their conversation had drifted outside. He walked inside. "Betty, did you say something about me being wise?" His eyes twinkled as he looked at her.

"And you have excellent hearing, too," Betty added.

He laughed.

"What are you doing out here?" Erin asked.

"It sounds as if you don't want me." He stood behind one of the kitchen chairs, looking from Betty to Erin with a wounded expression.

"What Daughter means is that your appearance is a surprise."

Sawyer studied her. Erin felt itchy under his

gaze, remembering how close they had come to a real kiss.

"Why are you here?" she asked.

His eyes danced. "I realized the last time I rode how much I missed riding."

Tate's door opened, and he walked out of his room. "I thought I heard you."

"I'm here to ride."

The thundercloud lifted from her brother's face. "I'd like that. C'mon, let's go saddle the mounts." Tate headed outside.

Sawyer's gaze met Erin's. "That okay with you?"

Relief flooded her and she smiled. "That's an excellent idea."

He stepped closer and whispered, "I thought your brother might need some guy time after being hauled around all week by women."

"Thank you," she whispered and had to stop herself from brushing a kiss across his cheek.

"It would've been okay with me if you'd done it."

Her heart raced as if he'd heard her thoughts.

He turned and walked outside, leaving Erin with her mouth hanging open.

Betty laughed. "I've never seen a man able to confuse you like that."

Starting to protest, Erin saw Betty shake her head. Erin snapped her mouth shut.

"Good. Truth is good."

* * *

Sawyer and Tate rode north of the ranch house.

Stopping his horse, Sawyer took in the harsh landscape. Range grass grew in clumps. Tree-like cacti and shorter cluster groups of cactus dotted the horizon along with rocks and boulders.

Tate pulled on the reins when he noticed Sawyer had stopped. "What are you looking at?"

"There's a rare beauty to this land."

Tate turned his mount around and rode back to where Sawyer sat. "Are you sure the folks at the rodeo haven't hit you in the head?"

Chuckling to himself, Sawyer understood what Tate asked. "I guess you might think me crazy, but I like this place. I feel it in my bones."

"Now I know you're nuts."

Sawyer lightly kicked his horse into motion. "Why would you say that?"

"Because you see how harsh this land is. What's the beauty in that?"

"The simplicity. The starkness. The colors."

Tate looked at the landscape again and shrugged. "If you say so."

They continued riding. The land dipped, and they walked their mounts down into the gully below.

"How'd the week go?" Sawyer asked.

Tate's lips tightened.

"Has your sister told you what's going on with the rodeo? Have you seen the website?"

"I looked. I'm surprised Sis could do that."

"She didn't. Traci did. And she worked with your sister on it."

Stopping his horse, Tate blinked at Sawyer. "Are you trying to pull something on me?"

"No. It made me do a double take, too. But this week, they've worked together on the website, getting it up and running."

"That's unreal."

"Proves you shouldn't lose faith."

"All I know is that I'm a laughingstock at school. Baby Tate is what they're calling me."

Stopping his mount, Sawyer leaned on the saddle horn. "What it proves is that you're a man who takes his punishment without complaining. Ignore the other guys. They know you ditched and were caught. Let their stupidity roll off your back. You know you're paying for what you did. Be proud of yourself. I am."

"Really?"

"You got it. I've been on the wrong end of different situations. Some were my mistakes. Others weren't. I'll admit, I had a mouth as a teen." Sawyer remembered the beatings he'd gotten. "It took a while for me to smarten up. When my mouth almost got me and my brother beaten to a pulp, I decided it was time to change.

"You strike me as a smarter guy than I was. It might look dark now, but God's in control."

"What if my dad dies? I mean when Mom

calls, she's always so cheerful, trying to hide Dad's condition, but I hear Auntie and Erin talking. They should be up-front with me. I mean Sis could pick me up after school and take me to see Dad."

The fear in Tate's voice punched Sawyer in the heart. "True, but a five-hour round trip is not something you could do during the week. Hey, the FaceTime exchanges are great. You get to see your parents."

Tate scowled.

"Sometimes moms try to shield their children." That was an experience Sawyer had never had. "Be up-front and honest with your mom. Tell her you worry more not knowing. She'll respond. Has your sister talked about what they think is going to happen?"

"No. When I saw Dad after the stroke, he was pretty out of it. I know he wanted Sis to take over for him."

"True, but I don't think your father would want you to spin out of control. You want to be able to face him and lift your head up high and say, 'I stood strong.'"

Tate didn't look sure, but he nodded.

"I wanted to ask you if you like the rodeo. Have a specialty?"

"I love trick riding. Sometimes I work with Dad and the other wranglers, but I haven't competed."

"You've got to do what you love."

Tate stopped and stared at him. "You mean you're not going to lecture me about tradition? I need to compete since my great-grandfather started the rodeo?"

"No."

After a moment of thinking, Tate nodded and started riding. They didn't say anything on the ride back to the barn.

"Who's that riding back into the corral with Tate?" Mary Morning Star Delong asked as she entered the kitchen.

Her mother's voice startled Erin so badly that all sorts of bad outcomes raced through her mind. Had something happened to her father? Erin jumped up from the table and ran to her mother's side. "Is Dad okay? Why didn't you tell us you were coming home?"

"Your father's condition has improved enough that the nurses encouraged me to go home and sleep in my own bed."

"So Dad's doing better? Talking and moving his arms and legs?" Erin's heart danced at the news.

"He is, and he asked about you and the rodeo." Her mom's eyes glistened with moisture.

Both Erin and Betty smiled.

"But no one has answered my question about the man who rode in with your brother. I assume that truck parked in our driveway is his."

Erin nodded. "Sawyer Jensen. He's the man the rodeo board hired to do the rodeo overhaul." Erin had avoided telling her mother details of her initial meeting with Sawyer.

Mary studied her sister, then daughter. "And what's he doing here?"

"He's been out riding with Tate," Erin answered.

"Is that wise?"

Mary barely stood five feet tall, and had lost her slender frame years ago, but anyone who thought Mary wasn't a force to be reckoned with hadn't met her.

"Mom, Tate hadn't said anything about Dad, but all anyone needed to do was look at him to know he is hurting. Sawyer stepped in to help. It's been good for Tate."

"It's true, Sister."

Before anyone could respond, the screen door opened and the men walked in.

Tate froze and Sawyer bumped into him. He reached out and steadied the teen.

Her mom didn't wait for her son to say anything, but embraced him. She whispered softly in Tate's ear in Navajo. He nodded.

Mary stepped back and studied Sawyer. Although the height difference should've been comical, somehow Erin saw equally matched opponents.

"I'm Mary Morning Star Delong. And you are?"

Sawyer took Mary's hand and met her probing gaze head-on. "I'm Sawyer Jensen. It's nice to meet you, ma'am. I hope everything is all right with your husband."

"Detrick is doing better and encouraged me to come home for the weekend. I decided my children needed to see their mother."

"I'm glad to hear it. You have a wonderful family." He didn't retreat under her scrutiny.

Mary nodded her head regally.

Erin knew more would come. No one moved, waiting for Mary to continue. "So, you are the man who won the contract over my daughter."

Her mother didn't disappoint Erin. No bitterness or anger tinged Mary's words, just strength to learn the truth. Ground rules were laid out.

Sawyer didn't shrink away; instead, he stood up straighter. "I am, but Erin and I have been working together, and she's pointed out some places where I needed to improve my plan."

Tate snorted. Betty harrumphed.

Mary glanced at her son as to stop any further "comments."

"So, you and my daughter are working together?"

"We are. And Erin and Traci have been collaborating this week on the website for the rest of the county to see and use."

"I see." Her mother turned to Erin, and Erin saw the countless questions she would have to answer. "Many things have changed."

"Yes, the world's been turned upside down," Betty commented.

Erin fought ducking her head. Suddenly, she felt exposed in a way she hadn't since she was six and dyed her mother's prize lamb green for Saint Patrick's Day.

"Stay for dinner with us, Sawyer," Mary said. "I would like to learn more of your plan and the working relationship you've developed with my children."

Her mother had *that* tone, which no one refused. "Thank you, ma'am. I appreciate the invitation, but I need to be back in town."

Shock ran through the kitchen from Erin and Tate to Betty and Mary. No one had ever refused Mary when she used that tone.

Mary quickly hid her reaction and studied him. Sawyer didn't squirm under her mother's penetrating gaze.

Slowly, acceptance filled Mary's eyes. "Then you must have Sunday dinner with us after church. I would like to learn more about you and what you are working on for the rodeo."

"I don't wish to be trouble, ma'am."

"Sometimes no matter how hard we try, we are. So stop fighting it and accept your role."

Sawyer blinked, then a smile curved his mouth. "I see the mother is as formidable as the daughter."

"Give in now," Tate said. "Your life will be

simpler." He snatched a piece of bread out of the bowl on the table.

"I'd be delighted." He nodded and walked out.

Erin followed Sawyer to his truck. When he heard the screen door slam, he paused and turned. "Is there something else?"

He stood there, open and ready to answer any of her questions.

She waited until she stood before him, not wanting her words to carry on the wind. "Thank you for reaching out to Tate."

Shrugging, he smiled down at her. "Like I told you before, I want to give to others the same help I got. Sometimes God puts you in a place, and you know you need to reach out."

"True." Oddly, Erin didn't want him to leave, yet. She wanted to talk to him about Tate or the way the rodeo was coming along, but she knew he needed to go. Stepping back, she said, "See you at church Sunday."

"I'll look forward to it and sitting in the pew next to you and listening to that lovely voice of yours."

She watched as Sawyer pulled away. No one had ever told her they liked her voice. She wanted to blush but knew she'd better keep those emotions under control unless she wanted to face her mother's questions. And, at this moment, she didn't want to talk about the feelings Sawyer inspired.

* * *

Sawyer looked through all the bids that had come in. He thought about the invitation he'd received from Erin's mother. He probably should've stayed, but he knew the family needed time to be alone and talk. Earlier, when he'd had dinner at Lulu's, the place had buzzed with excitement, and it just wasn't the usual Friday night joy for the weekend. Several people joined him at his table and talked about their bids and ideas on how to help with the rodeo redo. There were many good ideas, but he didn't know if he could rely on these people. Could they pull off what they proposed or were they simply ideas with no substance?

He wanted to talk to someone about it. He could call anyone on the board, but he finally admitted who he wanted to talk to. He dialed Erin's cell phone.

"Sawyer, is there anything wrong?" Erin asked before he could say anything.

"No. But when I had dinner at Lulu's, lots of people came up and talked with me. I had one business from Las Vegas that intends to bid on chute gates. I wanted to head over there tomorrow and look at their product. I thought we might go together to check them out, as well as some other vendors."

The line remained quiet. His thinly disguised excuse for a date flashed like a neon light. He held his breath.

"I'd like that."

His breath rushed out, and he could breathe again. "I'll be by there at nine."

"See you then." She hung up.

Had he heard a lightness in her voice?

"Stop it," he told himself. He was a thirty-year-old man acting like a boy with his first girlfriend.

But he couldn't help himself.

When Erin put her cell phone down, she looked up and saw her mother standing at the door to the study.

"Who was that?"

For some silly reason, Erin didn't want to acknowledge her caller. Somehow, she was afraid if she shared Sawyer's invitation, her delight might go away. "That was Sawyer. He wants to drive into Las Vegas tomorrow and see the work of some of the vendors who've applied to work on the rodeo. He wants my input."

Mary nodded. "That is good. So, are you going to go with him?"

"Yes."

Sitting on the couch, Mary patted the place beside her. Erin came to her mother's side. Mary touched her daughter's cheek and brushed back the strands of hair that had come loose from her braid. "He's a handsome man, Daughter. He seems strong enough to hold his own against you."

Erin felt as if someone had smacked her hard

on the back, leaving her breathless and disoriented. "Mom, I'm not looking for a boyfriend."

"I didn't say you were."

"Then why mention it?"

"Because you need someone."

Erin didn't know what to think. "What are you talking about?"

"I'm talking about being afraid to give in to your heart. This man seems to have a heart big enough to allow you to soar. I like what I've seen between him and Tate."

Erin stared at her mother, stunned. "What brought this on?"

Mary looked down at her hands. "My husband's sick. As I sat in that room with him and prayed for his recovery, I asked God how I would go on. I have been blessed with a wonderful man and realize how precious life is." Mary took her daughter's hands. "What I want for you is a man as good as your father. A man who's as strong as you, who can walk with your strength and know his own. And for your brother, I prayed for the maturity for him to deal with his father's illness. And when I saw Sawyer and Tate riding in, I knew that prayer had been answered."

Erin's mind floundered to understand what her mother was saying. "So you trust Sawyer?"

"I see that God has provided a way. I want to talk to the man, listen to his words. I want to know if he'll share his heart. But for now, he's helping your brother."

Erin squirmed. Surely this wasn't God's way. She'd lost her rodeo bid. "Did you know about the contract going to another person, Mom?"

Her mother shook her head. "Immediately after the board meeting, your father had the stroke. No one told me the results of the vote. I didn't know anything about what had happened until you called me and told me that Sawyer won."

Erin, her heart still hurting, whispered, "Why would Dad vote against me, Mom? He knew I wanted the job."

Mary gently squeezed Erin's hands. "I don't know, Daughter. I don't understand, either. Since your father has been in the hospital, the results of the vote never crossed my mind."

Erin blinked back tears. "I can't understand how Dad could vote against me. That's been the hardest part." Erin closed her eyes, fighting for control. "Mel delighted in rubbing it in."

Mary snorted. "Mel's heart is so closed I'm afraid there's not much left of it." Slipping her arm around her daughter's shoulders, Mary drew Erin close. "From what I've seen of the young man who won the contract, maybe God brought him into our lives to help. With your father's condition, the burden of doing the rodeo might have been too much. And it seems that your brother needed him, also. Help comes in strange ways. Accept it.

"He seems a good match for you. He's not afraid to stand up for himself."

Erin wanted to object, but realized how ridiculous that sounded. Town folks knew that any man who dated her had better speak up for himself, so when Andy had proposed and she'd refused, no one had been surprised.

"I can find my own man, Mother."

"I didn't say you couldn't, but understand that a smile or a soft word will not ruin your reputation of being a wise woman. People come to you for help in solving problems, wanting advice. Sometimes walking softly holds more power than brute strength. Obstacles can be conquered with honey. Soft words don't mean weakness, but a confidence, and sureness, in yourself, which will not retreat in the face of those who don't listen. A dependence on God to lead."

Erin blinked at her mother. Where was this coming from? "I will think on your words, Mother."

Mary stood. "That lesson took a long time for me to learn, but once I did, life fell into place." Mary brushed a kiss across Erin's cheek. "I look forward to talking with Sawyer on Sunday."

Sleep didn't come quickly for Erin, with her mother's words tumbling around her head, making her wonder at the truth.

Had she put up walls, hiding from others?

Was she running? And was she ready to stop? Could she give in to the desires of her heart concerning Sawyer? Her mother said she should follow those desires.

She mulled over the idea. What could it hurt except break her heart, but would it be worth it to have someone love her and share the burdens?

The next morning Sawyer pulled into the driveway of the Delong ranch. He walked to the back door and called out, "Mornin', is Erin ready?"

Betty motioned Sawyer inside. Mary and Tate sat at the table eating.

"Would you like some coffee?" Betty offered. "I also have my special coffee cake if you haven't eaten."

Before he could respond, Erin appeared in the kitchen. Dressed in jeans and a Western blouse, her hair flowed around her shoulders like a silken black cape. The belt buckle at her waist he recognized as the top barrel racer for one year. She also had on snakeskin boots. It matched his attire of western shirt, jeans and boots.

Erin looked at the people around the table. "Auntie, I'd like some of your coffee cake and a mug of coffee to go."

"Why don't you sit and eat with us, Daughter?" Mary asked.

From her reaction, Sawyer knew Erin didn't want to stay.

"Mom, we've got a lot to do today for the rodeo. We need to get going."

Mary didn't respond except for a knowing smile.

Erin grabbed two travel mugs and poured coffee. "Do you drink it black?" she asked Sawyer.

"Yup, straight up."

She put the top on his mug and handed it to him. Grabbing the creamer, she fixed her coffee. Betty handed her two pieces of coffee cake. "You're the best." Erin brushed a kiss on her auntie's cheek.

Pausing at the door, Erin walked to her mother's side and hugged her.

"Remember my words," Mary whispered.

Erin nodded.

"I agree with Sister," Betty added.

Tate frowned and looked from his mother to his aunt to Erin. "What's going on?"

Betty smiled. "Too bad life is wasted on the young."

"Huh?"

Sawyer opened the screen door and heard Betty say, "Love is in the air."

"Where?" Tate asked.

Both the older women laughed.

Erin marched to Sawyer's truck, trying to ignore the conversation going on in the kitchen, but Sawyer cocked his head and grinned.

Great, how was she going to explain what had just happened?

Chapter Nine

Sawyer finished the last of the coffee cake, licking the crumbs off his fingers. He laughed. "Oh, I'm going to want another piece of that when I get back." He took a swig of his coffee.

"Both Betty and my mom are great cooks. Unfortunately, I did not inherit their talent."

Sawyer took his eyes off the road and looked at her. "It strikes me that maybe you didn't want their talent."

Erin chuckled. "Wow, you nailed that. How'd you guess?"

"Both my brother and I did rodeo growing up. I think Caleb could've given me a run for my money, but he wanted a steady paycheck to support us, so he developed the talent of being the best pickup rider in the business. He's as good as me in saddle bronc riding and bull riding."

He could see her mulling over the crumbs he gave her. She nodded. "True. You're one of the few people who's ever guessed that I wasn't interested in cooking."

"We each have our talents, and your talent lies elsewhere." He threw her a grin. "You could evaluate failing companies and write up plans to save them. My professors would've loved working with you."

"That's an idea. I just finished my MBA from University of New Mexico in Albuquerque. I could add to my credentials."

"Ah, you're one of those number crunchers."

Her laughter filled the cab of the truck, delighting him. That first day, when she marched into the conference room, he never would've expected to hear her tease him. "Dad understood my talent, but Mom wanted me to be more like her. I can cook, but if you don't give a snort, then most of what you cook is average. You can't be something you're not."

"I hear you." He pointed to the floorboard between them.

"There, by your feet, is an accordion file with the bids we've received so far. I wanted to go over them with you."

She found the file between the front seats and opened it. They spent the drive to Las Vegas scrutinizing each bid and talking about the person or business who had submitted it.

They finished reviewing the submissions just as they entered the outskirts of the city.

"Would you mind if we went to my mother's jewelry shop before we attend to the rodeo business?" Erin asked.

"Your mother owns a jewelry shop? Why'd no one say anything?"

"Well, with the rest of our lives falling apart, it slipped my mind." She directed him through the streets of Las Vegas.

"Mother's other talents include jewelry making, weaving and gardening." Erin looked down at her lap.

From the slump of her shoulders, Sawyer guessed that Erin felt her lack of artistic talent made her feel inadequate. "Remember, we all have different paths to walk."

Her head jerked up, and her gaze collided with his. "You're sounding more and more like Auntie."

"She's showing me new ways."

"My mother has an abundance of artistic talent, but she can't add a line of numbers and cares nothing about keeping her books straight or dealing with payroll. And don't get me going about paying taxes or dealing with dissatisfied customers or paying suppliers in a timely manner. But, somehow, some way, Mom charms them, and they forgive her. I'm trying to get her to hire a full-time manager again so all she has to worry about are her creations."

"From what I heard from folks in town, you're

the person that straightens out problems and fixes mistakes."

She didn't reply, but he saw her consider his words.

"You've done that for your mom, haven't you?"

The answer shone clearly in her eyes.

"It doesn't matter."

Erin directed him to the part of Old Town that housed her mother's jewelry store. The long adobe structure had been built in the early 1900s, before statehood. The uneven wood walkway out front had borne countless feet that walked up and down the street.

They parked in front of the store. Before she could get out of the truck, he reached for her hand. "It does matter, Erin. Your mom's a smart woman, and if she wanted to, she could hire a manager to take care of those problems."

"She had one." She got out of the truck before he could ask any more questions.

Shame on you, Mary Morning Star Delong, Sawyer thought. Why had Erin's mother kept her daughter tethered to her? The woman he met the other day knew how to run a business. This didn't feel right.

Opening the door, she called out, "Hey, Joe, I'm here to take care of that problem Mom had with Mrs. Gonzales's necklace."

Joe appeared in the doorway that led to the

back room, situated behind the glass cases holding the different artisan's creations.

"Erin, what a wonderful treat to see you." He gathered her into a hug. He looked over her shoulder at Sawyer.

"Who do you have with you?"

Sawyer held out his hand and introduced himself.

"Joe Torres. How do you know Erin?"

"I'm working with her on the revitalization of the bicounty rodeo."

"I've heard about that. People are talking in town about it. Should be interesting to see."

Erin carefully explained about Sawyer's role in the rodeo. "Joe's been working with Mother for the last twenty years. He's the one who convinced Mom to start her own line of jewelry. When Joe's wife passed away, he sold his store and Mom bought it. He's been helping her on and off for the last couple of years. I've tried to get Joe to accept the job as manager, but all he wants is to spend time with his grandchildren."

Joe shook his head. "I'm glad to help straighten things out temporarily, but with those resorts in Taos wanting the pieces your mother contracted with them, and received a down payment for, things are tense. I understand your mother's heart, concentrating on your father first, but she needs to notify the customers and let them know what is going on. I don't doubt they will give her time."

"I know."

Erin and Joe sat behind the counter and discussed how to deal with things. Erin called the disgruntled customer and explained the situation.

"Give me a half hour to catch up on paperwork," she told Sawyer, then disappeared into the back.

Joe and Sawyer faced each other.

"How are things working out?"

Another defender. Sawyer's first impression of Erin had proved to be true. She was a strong woman, but she was not the kind he expected. "She's kept me on my toes and thrown me more surprises than I know what to do with. She has me dancing."

"And is this a problem?" Joe watched Sawyer carefully.

"No, it's not a problem, but if I think one thing, Erin comes up with another way to solve the problem. I'm learning to see her point."

Joe smiled. "The Delong women can have you doing things that you never expected. Of course, when my wife died, I wanted to lie down and die, too, but Mary wouldn't allow me to do that. She threw me a lifeline."

"Unusual women, both Mary and her daughter." Sawyer shrugged. "I could include Aunt Betty, too."

"True. She came into the shop one time, but I knew she held her own with her sister."

Sawyer told himself it was none of his business, but he opened his mouth and said, "Tell me, why does Mary hold her daughter for ransom with her finances?"

Joe sat back and studied Sawyer. "You are an observant man and the only person I know who sees that. Detrick refuses to acknowledge it, and none of Mary's family or friends find a problem with it. They just chalk it up to the artisan in Mary." He rubbed his neck.

"So, I'm not out of line with my conclusions?" Sawyer quietly said.

"No, you're on the mark. About a year ago, Mary called Erin to ask for help." He paused. "Erin earned her undergraduate degree in accounting then used her earnings from barrel racing to pay for her masters. She'd win enough for a year of school, take off and attend UNM in Albuquerque."

Sawyer smiled. "I know that story. I did that myself."

"With rodeo?" Joe asked.

"Yes." It amazed Sawyer that Erin and he had followed the same path to get their degrees. Maybe that's why he felt so connected to her.

"Ah, I see you understand. When Erin started writing her master's thesis, I retired from the store. Mary refused to hire a new accountant, complaining about how much work it was to keep the books, create and care for the store. Erin volunteered to help until her mother found someone to take my place.

"That was some time ago, and I've seen the toll it's taken on Erin. I don't know if Mary even knows she's doing it. Maybe she's afraid to let go. Mary aids many. The daughter follows in her mother's footsteps. Perhaps Erin needs an advocate." Joe stared at Sawyer.

Sawyer's skin prickled, and the hair on the back of his neck stood up. If he took up this challenge, lives would be changed. "That's a big job."

"It will require a strong man who can tackle the situation."

Sawyer felt every word. "I'm here to finish redoing the rodeo. I'm not qualified to meddle in people's lives."

"Yes, you are. Of all the people surrounding Erin, only you've seen the truth. Mary Morning Star knows how to hire an accountant and the problem would be solved, but she ignores it."

"You've seen the truth, too."

Joe folded his arms over his chest. "True, and I have thought to battle this situation, but my heart is a friend to Mary. Your heart speaks to Erin. You can choose to help her or walk away, but think carefully before you decide."

Suddenly, the world shifted. He stood in a place he had never expected to be.

"Joe," Erin's voice called out.

"Think about it," Joe whispered, then walked through the doorway to the back.

They enjoyed a lunch in an outdoor café on the edge of Old Town. The food was a fusion of Navajo and Spanish styles.

"What did you and Joe talk about?" Erin took a sip of her iced tea.

"He told me how he encouraged your mom to create pieces of jewelry and explained how they worked together."

His answer came quickly, but she felt there must have been more to the conversation. "Did he explain why he wouldn't come back and work with Mom?"

"I think he wants the freedom to live his life."

"I can't blame him."

"So, why doesn't your mother hire someone to take care of her business?" He took a chip from the basket on the table and scooped up some hot sauce.

"I've told her she needs to do that. She says she's been too busy to interview a manager. And now with Dad sick—" She shrugged.

"How long has this been going on?"

Erin considered how long she'd been running interference for her mom. As she thought, she realized this pattern had been going on since she started writing her thesis. Comprehension slammed into her. When her gaze collided with Sawyer's, she knew he saw the truth.

"Too long." Feeling duped, she asked, "Why would Mom do that?"

"I'm the wrong person to try to answer that question. My mom wasn't a mom."

Erin heard that same pain again. "What do you mean?"

He sat back in his chair. "After my dad died of a sudden heart attack, mom couldn't handle the grief. Her world dissolved in an instant. Dad had worked for another rancher and we lived in a house on the property, but with Dad's death, we had to leave." He paused, lost in the old memories. "Mom went from a woman who fed us and kept the house to a woman who couldn't make a decision without either my brother's or my input. When that wasn't enough, she started seeking out boyfriends. The first couple of guys were nice, but my mom smothered them."

A knot in her stomach formed.

"The more men left her, the needier she became. The men she attracted had the attitude of 'it's my way or the highway,' and that didn't sit well with two teenage boys."

Erin covered Sawyer's hand, which rested on the table.

"I was the one with a mouth. If one of my mother's boyfriends hit her, I spoke up. I got my face punched several times."

He looked down at their hands as if noticing them for the first time. "It wasn't uncommon for Mom's boyfriends to beat her, and I'd tried to stop it, but I'd get beat up in the process." He shook his head. "You'd think I'd have smartened up, but I couldn't ignore it."

"That speaks well of you."

"No, I was the stupid one. Mom's boyfriends would tear into Mom when it was only me there. They knew not to start their garbage when Caleb was home. Of course, Caleb was older and bigger than me."

He looked into her eyes. "Do you know what Mom would tell me afterward? It was my fault. If I hadn't annoyed so-and-so, then it wouldn't have happened. Can you believe that?"

Her heart ached. "No, I can't. Your mom was mentally off-balance."

He looked down at their hands. The waiter appeared, and Sawyer paid the bill.

On the way to the truck, he pulled Erin under a tree, out of the view of people on the patio and gathered her into his arms. "I didn't mean to unload on you like that."

Tilting her head back, she looked up at him. He'd mentioned before his brother had been declared an emancipated minor. "What caused your brother to file to be on his own and take you?"

"You caught my references?"

"Yes, and I wondered what had happened."

He pulled her closer and rested his chin on the top of her head. She knew he needed another sympathetic heart to share his story with.

"Caleb was at work after school at the feed store. Mom and her boyfriend were drunk and arguing over the TV. I was at the kitchen table doing homework. Mom told her boyfriend she didn't want to watch his stupid show." He stopped. "The next thing I knew, I heard a choking sound and her boyfriend yelling things I won't repeat. I raced into the next room and found him strangling Mom. She clawed at his face and his hands, but she was turning red."

"I barreled into the man, knocking him off her. She scooted away and watched as the man started in on me. I put up a fight, but he got a couple of good punches to my face, bloodying me up good. When he drew back his hand to deliver the final blow—and I sometimes wonder if that blow would've been my last—it never came. My brother stood over me, like some kind of guardian. He told Mom's boyfriend if he wanted to beat someone up, try someone his own size.

"The man backed down and told us to get out. When we looked at Mom, she agreed with her boyfriend. We ran out the back door."

Her heart broke at Sawyer's mother's betrayal. When he looked down, Erin pulled back and saw wet spots on his shirt. She hadn't realized she cried.

She cupped his face. "I'm sorry."

He shrugged. "I told you about my mother so you could see that in the grand scheme of things your mother's actions are what I consider minor. I like Mary, but when we got to her jewelry store, something didn't feel right. Joe also knows that, for some reason, your mom is pulling you back to her."

She wanted to argue, but everything he said made sense. What's more, Erin already knew the truth he had told her; she just hadn't wanted to admit it to herself.

"So, you're not offended that I put my nose in your business?" He gently held both her arms above the elbows.

"No." Her mother's words rang in her ears. God had sent Sawyer to help their family. Her mother wasn't going to be pleased with his words. She rose up on her toes and tried to brush a kiss across his cheek, but he turned his head and their mouths met.

Shock raced through her. She should've pulled back, but she didn't. His arms slid around her waist. The warmth of his embrace and sweetness of his mouth soothed her heart. When he drew back, he looked down at her tenderly.

"I shouldn't have done that."

"True." Her eyes danced with joy.

He dropped his arms and stepped away. "Why don't we finish our business here in Vegas, then drive to Albuquerque and talk to the concrete manufacturer? I'd like to meet with him face-to-face, but I'll need to call him now and give him a heads-up."

Glancing down at her watch, she knew they had plenty of time. "I'm up for it."

"Then let me call him and arrange things."

It took only moments for Sawyer to set up the meeting. When he hung up, he grinned like a schoolboy, but he was a responsible adult. "It's set. C'mon, let's finish our business here then go to Albuquerque. We have a man to meet with."

"And while we're there, I'd like to stop by the hospital and see my dad."

"Absolutely."

As they drove to Albuquerque, Sawyer couldn't find his bearings from all that had transpired that morning. He knew any questions about the bids could be answered honestly by Erin. The woman had a good sense of people and honestly appraised each bid. He found he could count on her.

That truth blindsided him. She was the first woman he'd ever trusted in that deep a way. When he saw what was going on at her mother's jewelry store and told her, she had listened to him. She hadn't called him names or accused him of wanting to ruin her mother's name, but realized the legitimacy of what he said.

He had told the truth and she'd listened. That

was the first time he'd encountered that with a woman so close to him. He could honestly talk to her and she could deal with it, even if it wasn't an easy revelation. More than just admiration, he felt her pain and tried to relieve it.

Of course, he'd had no business kissing her, but he hadn't expected her to put her lips in front of his. That was an accident, but he wanted to repeat the happy accident.

As he glanced at her, his heart swelled. Erin was the first woman he had told about his mother. He remembered when he'd met his future sister-in-law and she'd confided that his brother had shared stories about their tough upbringing. That was when Sawyer knew something was up with Caleb and Brenda.

Was he in that same boat?

"What are you smiling at?"

Erin's voice jerked him to the here and now. "I was thinking about my brother and his wife. You met Brenda when you attended the rodeo there in Peaster last Memorial Day. She took over putting it on."

"I remember her. We talked a little about how she organized the rodeo. Of course, what our rodeo needed was an update."

"She's an amazing lady. She was a captain in the army until she was injured when a bomb went off in the café she was at in Baghdad."

"I didn't know."

"She's more than tough enough to handle my brother. It's nice to see her boss him around." He grinned. "You would understand and appreciate her methods of doing things."

She turned to him, and her solemn look made him nervous. Finally her lips twitched, and a wide smile creased her mouth. "Are you calling me bossy?"

"If the shoe fits." His light tone matched hers.

Waving away his comment, she said, "We talked about the problems we've had with our rodeo. I got some good ideas from her, but didn't implement them. The board hired you."

"And do you regret it?" He really wanted to know.

Her mouth turned up at the corners. "Ask me when we finish the rodeo."

"It's a date." And as the words died in the truck cab, he knew it would be a *date*.

Chapter Ten

The meeting with the concrete contractor opened their eyes. Erin now stared down at the invoice for the last work the contractor had done for the rodeo. Twenty-five hundred dollars. The price listed on Mel's final expense statement, which he dropped off at the office, was for thirty-five hundred and eighty-four dollars.

"It's unbelievable," she murmured. Mel had always been hard to get along with, but to embezzle—she never would've thought he'd do that.

"It happens," Sawyer said, bringing her back to the here and now. They sat in Sawyer's truck in front of the concrete manufacturer.

"Mel's known to be difficult. Too big for his britches, as my mother always likes to say." She studied him. "Have you run into this sort of thing before?"

"Yes. As long as there are people, we'll have things like this crop up."

Erin looked at the numbers on the photocopy of the check. "Surely there's another explanation," she whispered.

"What would you like to do now?"

"I'd like to go see my dad in the hospital since we're here," she said, without looking at Sawyer.

He didn't respond.

"What's wrong?"

"Are you going to ask your dad about the discrepancy now? You don't want to upset him."

She turned toward him. "I won't do anything to harm my dad," she said forcefully, "but I wonder if he suspected something." Her last words trailed off.

"Maybe that was the reason he brought in an outsider," Sawyer offered. "If I tripped over the discrepancy, others would be more inclined to believe me than you. It could be chalked up to bad feelings between you and Mel. I know Traci would've gone with that explanation."

That was it. Her heart and soul latched on to the reason for her father's actions. "You're right. No one would've believed me, but—"

"With me discovering it, others would know I didn't make it up."

Her gaze fell to the copy of the check in her lap again, making sure she wasn't dreaming. "That's true." She hadn't understood her dad's actions, but with this explanation things made sense. "Let's go to the hospital and see."

Reaching over, he squeezed her hand. His unconditional support made her heart sing with joy in the middle of this mess. She felt heaven's direction in the midst of this madness—something to hold on to. No, *someone* to hold on to.

Mary Morning Star stood beside her husband's bed. When Erin and Sawyer walked into the room, she smiled at them.

"Mom, what are you doing here?" Erin asked. "You just came home."

"Tate needed to see his father. I thought you and Sawyer had gone to Las Vegas."

"We did, then did some rodeo business here."

Erin walked to her father's bed. Picking up his hand, she gently cradled it. "Hello, Dad."

"Erin," Detrick choked out.

"It's good to see you face-to-face instead of just on the iPad. You've had us so worried."

Detrick's eyes went from Erin to Sawyer. He saw the question in the older man's gaze as it traveled from Erin to Sawyer.

"I wanted…" Detrick started.

"Dad, don't worry about anything." Erin stroked his forehead, brushing away a tear. "I believe in you, and I know you had your reasons for your vote. I trust you."

Sawyer felt awkward watching the tender scene play out between father and daughter. Mary stepped to his side. "When Erin told me that my husband voted for you, I knew he hadn't betrayed her. Never in the years we've been married has he deceived his family." She looked up into Sawyer's face.

"I think you're right. Your husband had a reason to bring me in."

Her eyes narrowed. "Something has happened."

"We may have stumbled on to some information that could be explosive."

"I knew it."

Erin caught Sawyer's hand and pulled him forward. "Dad, this is Sawyer. I don't know if you've met him in person before."

The older man shook his head. "Read his plan." The uttering of the words exhausted him.

"Erin's been very helpful. A little bossy, but a valuable asset." Sawyer didn't want to upset the old man with the truth they'd uncovered, but Sawyer suspected he already knew.

"True," Detrick whispered.

Mary took her husband's other hand and gently smoothed his hair back from his face.

"You let Sawyer and Erin take care of the rodeo. What you need to do is get well."

"That's true." Erin ran the back of her fingers over her dad's cheek. "Sawyer's come out to the ranch and ridden your mount. He and Tate have gone riding a couple of times. Tate's not drowning in a sea of estrogen with Sawyer there."

Erin looked around. "Where are Tate and Betty?"

"They are with Kai, eating. We'll drive back after they finish their meal."

A smile spread across Detrick's face as he traded looks with Sawyer. He read a thank-you in the older man's eyes.

The door opened.

"Good evening, Mr. Delong," the nurse called out. "I've got your evening pills here."

Sawyer's blood turned cold. He never thought he'd hear that voice again.

Mary turned and greeted the nurse. "Good evening, Sylvia."

"I see you didn't follow my advice and stay at home this weekend," Sylvia replied.

"Tate needed to see his father, but I promise to go home tonight."

"You will not help him if you wear yourself out. He's going to need all the support he can get once home."

Mary accepted the gentle chiding.

Slowly, Sawyer turned and came face-to-face with his mother. When she saw him, she momentarily froze.

The rest of the world faded away, and his past

came roaring back, nearly flattening him. He locked his knees to stay standing.

His mother recovered quickly and turned to Mary. "The doctor's here now and wants to talk to you. I'll get him."

"Do you think we can take Detrick home soon?"

"You'll need to talk that over with the doctor. I'll let him know you're here."

Sawyer didn't say anything as he stepped back to get out of everyone's way. The name tag on his mother's uniform said Carter. Where she'd gotten that name, he didn't know. The last he knew, her boyfriend's surname was Braddock. How many men had she gone through since him?

Sylvia glanced at him. "Who do you have with you, Mary?" Her voice cracked.

"This is Sawyer Jensen. He's working with our county rodeo board to revitalize our rodeo."

"He's a turnaround consultant," Erin added. She turned to him and smiled. But all Sawyer could see was his mother's face, and a flood of different, hard memories flowed in.

"It's nice to meet you, Sawyer." She gave him a tentative smile and nodded her head. Deep in her eyes he saw doubt and uncertainty.

He didn't trust himself to open his mouth. He simply nodded.

Both Mary and Erin glanced at him.

"Excuse me," he said, not trusting his reactions, and walked out of the room.

He didn't stop at the end of the hall. He walked to the exit and descended the stairs to the main floor. Emerging from the stairwell, he saw the door to the ground-level garden for the patients and families and pushed it open.

In one corner, he found a bench shaded by the building and sat, trying to regain his footing. He never thought he'd see his mother alive again. He'd often wondered what had happened to her. She hadn't bothered to contact her sons once she'd hit them up for money right after Caleb had been declared an emancipated minor. They'd moved away and settled in the small city of Plainview, south of Lubbock. Sawyer doubted his mother had ever tried to discover what had happened to her sons.

They had grown into manhood despite their mother's actions, and both his brother and he imagined she was probably dead.

As he thought about it, his mother looked like a woman in charge of her faculties. She certainly had to be in order to be a nurse in the hospital.

He frowned. A nurse? When had that happened? Before his dad died, his mother had always taken care of her boys when they were sick, and she had a talent for making them feel better. She looked as if she had a peace about her, which brought him to the million-dollar question—what had happened in his mother's life?

* * *

"Thank you, Doctor," Mary replied to the doctor's final assessment.

"I'll look for a rehab center closer to home," Mary told him. "I think going home for his rehabilitation would help my husband."

"If you need anything else, be sure to have the nurses contact me." The doctor left the room.

Mary turned to her husband and smiled down into his face. "It's good news, husband. It will take work on your part to get you back to your old self, but I don't doubt you can do it." Mary cupped his cheek. "My heart nearly stopped, and your children have not known what to do, so you need to work hard to get better. And Tate needs you more than ever."

Detrick nodded.

"I'll look around, Mother, for a place closer to home," Erin said.

"All that is important is that your father gets well. Oh, I have one more question for the doctor." Mary hurried out into the hall.

Erin stepped to her father's side and grasped his hand. His eyes held a question.

"What is it?"

He glanced toward where Sawyer had stood.

"Are you wanting to talk about Sawyer?"

He nodded. Talking took effort, and he tired easily.

"I will say I didn't understand why you voted

for someone else, but as the days go by, I see that vote in a different light." She squeezed her father's hand. "Sawyer and I have found some discrepancies in the last budget done for the rodeo update."

He squeezed her hand again.

"As we've talked about it, I realized if Sawyer found the discrepancy, others would believe him quicker than me."

Detrick's body relaxed.

"Is that it?"

He blinked and tried to speak, but the sounds coming out of his mouth weren't intelligible.

"It shook my faith, but I knew you had a reason."

A tear ran from the corner of her dad's right eye. She wiped it away.

There were other things she wanted to talk to her father about—how Sawyer had reached out to Tate and how she'd found herself enjoying her skirmishes with him—but now wasn't the time.

The door opened again, and Erin turned, expecting Sawyer. It was her mom.

"I'm going to find Sawyer and go home. Don't stay too late, Mom. We might tire out Dad."

"Ah, now it happens, the child is trying to become the parent," Mary replied.

"No, it's a daughter who is worried about her mother's safety." Leaning over, Erin kissed her mom's cheek and thought about asking her mother why she kept ignoring her accounts at the store, but now wasn't the time to confront her. Tomorrow they'd talk.

Walking out of the room, Erin looked for Sawyer. He wouldn't have left, but she did not see him. At the nurse's desk, she asked Sylvia, "Have you seen Sawyer?"

Sylvia's hand jerked on the computer keyboard. When she glanced up, she took a deep breath. "No, I haven't seen him on the floor. Would he have left?"

Erin rubbed her neck. "Not without me. We drove together from home."

Erin started to the elevator doors.

"Have you known him long?" Sylvia asked.

Erin turned. "No. He won the bid over me to take our failing rodeo and turn it around. I wasn't happy to have lost, but I will say he's much different than I expected."

"How so?"

Erin shrugged. "Well, first of all, the man's a cowboy who has won a championship belt buckle, so he knows his stuff. We don't have some egghead who thinks he knows what a cowboy and his horse need. Sawyer's lived it. But what's amazed me is that he's listened to my input to his plan." A laugh escaped her. "I might have lost the bid, but I wasn't going to walk away from our rodeo and let this stranger have free rein over it." She smiled.

"And he's been helpful with my seventeen-

year-old brother." Suddenly Erin couldn't stop
the words rushing out of her mouth. Here was
the nurse who'd been with them from the beginning, who could give an unbiased opinion or at
least a reasonably unbiased one. "Tate wouldn't
talk to any of us women about Dad's stroke, but
somehow Sawyer understood his turmoil.

"And for that I'm grateful." Erin shook her
head. "With all the upheaval and craziness going
on around the ranch, Sawyer recognized a lost
teenage boy and reached out to him. When the
sheriff called me about my brother ditching
school, my first reaction was to rain all over him,
but Sawyer talked me out of it. He's surprised me
with his keen perception of the situation. Most
men wouldn't follow through like he did, but he's
gone riding with Tate and they've talked a couple of times."

"That's amazing for a stranger to do." Sylvia
picked up a pen. "Sometimes what we think is
the end is a turn in the road we didn't expect."

Erin had the strangest feeling that Sylvia wasn't
talking about her situation now. The words came
from experience.

A buzzer from one of the patient's rooms took
Sylvia in a different direction. Erin walked to the
elevator doors. Before she could push the but-
ton, the doors slid open and Sawyer emerged. He
looked around. "Are you ready to leave?"

"Yes. When I didn't see you out here, Sylvia,

the nurse, asked if you'd left without me. I told her no, that you'd driven me."

"I'm sorry. I went downstairs for a moment."

She waited for more of an explanation but didn't get it.

"Are you ready to leave?" The tone of his voice was flat.

The more he spoke, the more suspicious she became. "Yes."

With the exception of a Western music station out of Albuquerque playing on the radio, the ride home passed in silence.

Erin knew something had changed at the hospital, but she couldn't figure out what.

"I'm encouraged by how good Dad looks," she said, hoping to get a conversation going.

"Uh-huh."

"And I'll talk to Mother about her bookkeeping."

"That's good."

"And I think I'll ride my horse right into church tomorrow to liven things up."

"That's a good approach."

She turned and faced him head-on. It took him several minutes to realize she had stopped talking. When he looked her direction, he said, "What?"

"Where are you, Sawyer? Because you're not here with me in this truck."

"Things piled up on us today, and I'm just trying to sort them out." He looked back to the interstate.

His explanation could've been the truth, but she had this feeling in her gut it wasn't the entire reason he was so far removed from her. She didn't try again. The words of caution he'd offered before about Tate rang again in her head. *Don't push.*

It went against her nature. She wanted answers, to sort out the situation now, but something inside her warned her, and for the balance of the drive, nothing was said.

He pulled into the ranch driveway. Following her out of the truck, he caught up with her in a couple of steps and caught her hand.

"Are you okay?" He studied her face.

"Yes. Are you?"

He pulled her into his arms and held her close, resting his chin on the top of her head. His hand rubbed her back. She found comfort in his action, but wondered if he didn't need the comfort, too.

"It's been a long day and seeing your dad was hard, I know."

She noticed he didn't answer her question. Instead, he cupped her face and gently kissed her. It wasn't a kiss of passion but of comfort and solace. He brushed another kiss across her lips. "I'll see you tomorrow."

She stared after his retreating form, wondering what was going on with him, because she didn't have a clue.

Chapter Eleven

Sawyer stared at the ceiling trying to find his way through the maze of conflicting emotions. It'd been a roller coaster of a day, from this morning around the Delong table with coffee and inquisitive minds, to the joy of talking with Erin about the bids that had come in, to his discovery of her mother's use of her. Erin had honestly listened to him without any recriminations.

Her reaction rocked him back on his heels, but the coup de grâce was meeting his mother face-to-face in Detrick's room at the hospital. His knees had nearly buckled when he'd heard her voice. He thought he might be hallucinating, but when he turned, it was his mother—a better, healthier version of his mother, much like she'd been when his father was alive. But there was something more in her demeanor that puzzled him.

What was it? She didn't seem nervous or

unsure. She moved with confidence. A woman at peace.

That thought blew him away.

The nurse in Detrick's room physically resembled his mom, but she'd changed from the inside out.

He should call his brother and tell him what had happened, but he wasn't ready to talk to Caleb.

Sawyer thought about calling Pastor Garvey in Plainview to talk to him, but what would he say? He saw a woman who was a dead ringer for his mom but acted nothing like the woman he'd known. Besides, his mother wasn't a nurse.

People can change, the thought came.

He rested his head in his hands and ran his fingers through his hair. He needed to know more before calling his brother.

Erin walked into the kitchen, where her mother stood making her special honey cake for breakfast before church.

"Did you and Sawyer finish the business you had in Las Vegas yesterday before you came to the hospital?" Mary asked. "You didn't mention anything about how things went."

"We worked while on the road to Vegas and dropped by your store."

"You two agreed on what needs to be done."

Mary looked up from the bowl with a knowing smile.

"We have. Sawyer's an insightful man."

Mary smiled. "Did you ask him if he is part Navajo?"

Erin hoisted herself onto the counter and stole a few raisins from a bowl.

"No, I didn't ask him about that, but he asked me why I was doing your books at the store since you're such an insightful and capable woman, and why you didn't hire a bookkeeper or buy a software program that would track your sales and expenses instead of drafting your daughter into doing your books."

Mary paled. "What did you say?"

"I blinked at Sawyer, realizing, for the first time, that he was right about what was happening."

Mary pulled out a chair from the table and sat down. Erin jumped off the counter and squatted in front of her mother.

"What has frightened you, Mother?"

Mary cupped Erin's cheek, and her eyes glistened with moisture. "I realized that my firstborn was now a grown and very capable woman who had earned her undergraduate degree and is close to getting her masters." Mary took a breath. "I guess I feared you would feel you no longer need your mother and leave to make your own way. I didn't want to face that."

Rising up on her knees, Erin wrapped her arms around her mother. "I will never outgrow my need for you. But I know you want to see me spread my wings and fly. You and Father made that possible. Everything was possible. If I could think it, I could try it. I knew this because of you and Father. Never did you put any limits on my imagination. I've talked with other girls in college and heard how they were directed in the way their families wanted them to go, never paying attention to their daughter's strengths. I found this so foreign and wasteful of their talents. I appreciated my parents even more."

"So much has changed," Mary whispered.

"True, but you always said there is a merciful Lord who walks with us."

Mary laughed through her tears. "There is nothing more humbling than having to live by one's own words."

"Sometimes we forget and need to be reminded." Erin gently wiped the tears from her mother's cheeks.

Betty walked into the kitchen. She looked at them and asked, "What is going on?"

"The sharing of wisdom, Sister, and the reminder to live with one's words with grace."

Betty looked from her sister to her niece and frowned. "What?"

Erin stood and wrapped her arm around her aunt, drawing her close.

Mary took a deep breath. "My daughter called me out on trying to keep her close. She assured me her love will continue, no matter where she is."

Understanding lit Betty's eyes. "It's hard, Sister, to let the first one go. Talk to me, I will help."

"Thank you, Auntie."

Sawyer slipped into the back of the church. He'd overslept and thrown on his clothes and dress shirt. He'd missed the song service. Instead of parading down the aisle, making a show of himself, he sat in the next to the last pew and listened to the sermon. The preacher spoke about forgiveness and said that if you forgave the person who wronged you, that forgiveness would free you. No longer would you have to carry around the crippling weight that ate your soul.

Sawyer's gaze drilled a hole into the pastor. Obviously, the man didn't know what he was talking about. He hadn't had to sleep out in the field behind his house when his mother entertained her drunk boyfriend who was spoiling for a fight.

"Let loose and let God heal your heart."

Sawyer folded his arms over his chest, throwing up a barrier. His heart and head weren't interested.

The pastor said the final prayer, and the organist played the closing hymn.

As people filed out, Sawyer didn't move from his place on the pew, still struggling with the message.

Tate sat beside him. "You plan to sit here all day? Church's over. I thought you were eating with us."

When Sawyer looked around, he saw Erin, her aunt and mother standing at the end of the pew. They'd witnessed his struggle.

Fighting his awkwardness, he stood and pasted on a smile. "I'm ready."

Mary cocked her head, studying him, as if she could read his confused heart. She nodded.

"I'll follow you to the ranch," Sawyer told them. "I'd be more than willing to have Tate ride with me."

Within minutes, they were on the road.

"Sis was worried that you might not show up today."

Sawyer shot a glance at Tate. "She say why?"

"No. But she kept looking down the aisle while we were singing."

"I overslept."

"I hear you. One time I slept through my alarm for school and managed to get ready in five minutes. Amazed my mom and sister. Dad knew I could pull it off." At the mention of his father, Tate seemed to deflate.

"Your dad looked good yesterday at the hospital."

"Yeah, he did when I saw him, but Sis acted

kinda strange when she came in last night. I thought something had happened with Dad."

Hearing Tate alerted Sawyer that Erin had picked up on his agitation. "We did a lot yesterday. I think the relief your sister had after seeing your dad made her a little—uh—"

Tate grinned, waiting to hear Sawyer's explanation. "Yes?"

"Off," he said, finally committing to a word. "But I expect you to keep this conversation between us."

"You bet." The kid folded his arms over his chest and kept grinning.

"Anything I need to know before your mom questions me?" Sawyer asked on the drive.

Tate stroked his chin. "Just be straight-up honest with her."

"I hear ya."

"I know. Believe me, I've never gotten anything by my mom, and I've tried."

Sawyer laughed. He could see Tate trying to put something over on Mary. It was nothing like his experience with his own mom, who had managed not to be aware that her boys were even in the house.

"But Mom's fair."

Sawyer wondered how fair Mary would be since he won the contract over her daughter. So far she'd been reasonable, but he hadn't spent much time with her. He knew his mom would've been out for his hide if he'd won over the person she wanted to get the job. Her sons weren't necessarily the people she backed.

The ranch house came into view. Tate's prediction would soon be put to the test.

Erin threw her purse on the desk in the kitchen and walked to the sink to wash her hands.

"How are you, child?" Mary asked, stopping next to Erin. Her mom had been watching her all through church. Erin felt guilty, but for what?

"I'm fine." Her clipped response gave away the truth—she wasn't—but before her mother could pursue the topic, Tate and Sawyer walked in. Mary leaned close. "We'll talk later. We have much to discuss."

They'd already talked. What now? Erin turned and walked away. It took less than five minutes for them to get dinner on the table, and then Mary motioned for them to take their seats. Sawyer sat next to Tate and across from Erin.

After a prayer, Betty dished out a lamb stew and placed a piece of blue corn bread on the edge of the bowl.

It took a moment of Sawyer studying the bread to ask, "Is this supposed to be this color?"

"It's Auntie's favorite blue corn bread. Try it," Tate urged.

Sawyer had eaten worse. He took a bite and

slowly chewed the corn bread. The sweet taste of the cornmeal raced over his tongue. "That's good."

"Of course, so how was your trip to Las Vegas yesterday?" Betty asked.

Erin looked at her mother. "We got a lot of things ironed out at Mom's shop and with the different people working with the rodeo."

They discussed how Detrick looked and the plans for this next week. They'd noticed a weakness on her father's left side, which they talked to the doctor about.

"On the way home from church, Sawyer said he'd like to ride this afternoon." Tate turned to Erin. "Want to go with us, Sis?"

Erin liked the enthusiasm her brother displayed. More like the old Tate. Glancing at Sawyer, she saw him nod at her.

"You're more than welcome to join us, Erin."

Oddly enough, she wanted to go out with them. "A ride this afternoon sounds like a good idea."

"So, you are a championship rider, Sawyer?" Mary accepted her bowl of stew.

"Yes, ma'am. I won my buckles the summer of my freshman year in college. When I first got this job, Erin wanted to make sure I understood the needs of the men and women who compete in rodeo, so she questioned me."

Nodding, Mary said, "I'm sure she did."

Erin refused to look at anyone.

"My daughter has a heart for others and wanted to make sure those needs were addressed."

"Mom, Sawyer doesn't need to hear that."

"I've seen that strength myself," Sawyer answered.

Erin's head jerked up, and she saw him smile.

"And, I know her single-mindedness." He grinned, letting her know he was enjoying himself.

"Odd you should say so. Erin said the same thing about you."

"Mom," Erin protested.

Mary smiled calmly. "He complimented you, Daughter. He should know you hold him in the same regard."

Nothing like having your mother reveal your deepest secrets.

Sawyer's eyes twinkled when they met hers. "I guess that's why we get along so well."

Her heart fluttered. Sawyer was right. They understood each other on a deeper level. She had never felt this way about another man, and she didn't know exactly what to do with the feeling. Across the table, her mother and Aunt Betty grinned like satisfied cats.

Suddenly, Erin wanted to laugh, and, with her heart light, she couldn't wait to get out on the range, with the horse beneath her and Sawyer and Tate by her side.

* * *

The three of them rode west of the house. The high desert slowly descended to a small creek that ran through the property. The horses picked their way down the ridges left by previous flash floods.

The wind increased, and the clouds turned a greenish-gray color and looked as if someone had a giant hand mixer, churning them.

Her skin pricking at the sight, Erin said, "We should probably head back."

"Let's get to the river, then we can turn back," Tate replied. "It's not that far."

Sawyer and Erin traded looks. In this part of New Mexico, storms were notorious for rolling in at an amazing speed, and they should turn around and head to the ranch, but for the first time in a long time, Erin saw her brother smile and joke, so she pushed aside her misgivings. At the river, they allowed the horses to rest and drink.

Thunder rolled across the prairie, shaking the ground where they stood. Their horses started to dance with nervousness.

Sawyer stroked his horse's neck. "Your sister's right, and we should start back. Our mounts sense something coming in."

Tate didn't protest. Having ridden all his life, he knew to listen to his horse and the weather around. They mounted up and headed back. Starting up one of the sandy hills, a gust of wind hit Tate, and his mount lost his footing and stumbled backward, rolling over. Tate flew through the air and landed against a large rock. Erin and Sawyer dismounted and ran to him.

Sawyer got there first and gently rolled him over. Tate cried out. Looking at the odd position of his arm, Sawyer realized it was broken. The force of the wind pushed her into Sawyer. He caught her, steadying her. "You okay?"

Erin braced herself against his shoulders. "Yes."

Lightning flashed across the sky, with the roar of thunder immediately following. Tate moaned and opened his eyes.

"Tate, how are you?" she asked.

"My head hurts and my arm."

Sawyer looked around at the darkening horizon, taking in the swirling black clouds. "Normally, I'd say to wait for EMS, but with that storm barreling down on us, we can't."

"Can you get Tate up on his horse?" Erin asked.

"Yes." Sawyer scooped the teen up and put him in his saddle.

"Do you feel you can ride by yourself?" Sawyer asked.

"Yeah."

"You sure?"

The teen nodded, but his lips tightened, going white.

As Erin and Sawyer mounted their horses, another burst of wind hit them, peppering them with sand and debris. Something slammed into her upper arm, making her shout in pain. When she looked at Sawyer, he'd slumped forward against the neck of his horse. Tate still sat in his saddle, but he didn't look steady.

"Sawyer," Erin called, but the roar of the wind swallowed her cry. Awkwardly dismounting, she went to Sawyer's side. He'd been knocked out cold, and a trickle of blood ran down the side of his face. Thankfully he'd kept his seat, slumping against the horse's neck. Her dad's horse, Duke, didn't rear, instead remaining steady and bearing Sawyer's weight.

She grabbed Duke's reins and wrapped her horse's reins around her jeans' belt loop. "Easy, Duke." She tried to reassure the horse, laying her hand on the horse's neck. "You're an amazing pro." Her right upper arm burned like fire, but she moved to Sawyer's side. A tree branch lay a little beyond where Duke stood. Had that hit Sawyer? The blood that had trickled down his face had stopped. She took off her belt and gathered Sawyer's hands around the horse's neck, anchoring Sawyer's wrists together.

"I'm depending upon you, Duke, to get him back." She took the reins of her brother's horse. "You think you can stay on the horse yourself or do you want me to ride behind you?"

"I don't know, Sis."

"Okay, we'll try me riding behind you."

She tied Duke's reins to the saddle of her brother's horse, then gathered Dancer's reins in the other hand and mounted behind Tate. The pain in her shoulder made the horizon go a little fuzzy, but she drew in a deep breath. "Is this going to work for you?" She saw the doubt and fear in his eyes, but he nodded. "You can grab my arm to steady yourself."

"Okay."

Lord, help, she prayed as she started the group home.

She carefully picked their way up the wash and gained the high ground. Once up on the prairie, the wind buffeted them. Sawyer remained hunched over his horse's neck, and Tate clutched her arm. Erin wanted to gallop, but keeping Sawyer and Tate on their horses was her main priority.

Suddenly the skies opened up and it started raining, drenching them to the skin. Sawyer moaned and started to move. She guided her horse to Duke. Laying her hand on Sawyer's back she called out, "Stay still."

He quit moving.

As the horses walked, she kept checking on Sawyer and Tate.

"I'm not going to make it, Sis."

"Yes, you are. You're part of *the people* and will not let a little rain storm stop you."

The horse stepped in a gully, jerking her and Tate. He yelled and went slack against her. A jolt of pain shot through her shoulder, making her see stars. When Tate started to slump, she wrapped her arm around his waist to steady him. She tried not to jostle his arm but hit it, causing him to moan.

She would make it, she told herself, fighting the pain and blackness crowding her vision. They all would.

It seemed like an eternity before the ranch house came into view. When she rode into the yard with two injured males, her mother and aunt raced out the back door.

"What happened?" her mother shouted.

"The wind managed to take out both Tate and Sawyer." Erin winced as she walked the horses into the barn. Her mother grabbed the reins.

"I think Tate's arm is broken."

Her mother and Betty reached up for him. Erin helped slide her brother off the horse as carefully as they could. She slowly dismounted with her shoulder protesting. Walking to Duke, she untied Sawyer's hands, and the three women tried to maneuver him gently to the ground, but with his weight and momentum, he crashed into Erin, knocking her backward, and then the lights went out.

Erin woke in the emergency room, looking up at the white-tiled ceiling.

"Good, you're awake." A man in a white lab coat and scrubs looked down at her.

"Where am I?"

"You're in the university hospital in Albuquerque. You suffered a dislocated shoulder, and after we popped it back into place, it appears something else happened to your shoulder. You have a nasty cut and deep bruise. Trying to support your brother's weight wasn't a good idea."

Memories of the afternoon came into focus. "I didn't have a choice. I couldn't leave my brother and Sawyer in that wash at the mercy of the storm."

"True, and I heard you're quite a hero."

She didn't feel like one. "Where are they?"

"The men who came in with you are both stable."

"I'd like to see them."

The doctor hesitated.

"The younger man is my brother."

"I know. He's in one of the other emergency bays."

She tried to get up but gasped at the pain. The doctor helped her lie back down. "Let the nurse tend to your arm before you go trotting off."

"Are my mom and aunt here?"

"No, they haven't made it. The helicopter was only able to bring in the three injured patients. Can you tell me what happened, so I know some background on the other two patients?"

She described what had happened on their ride.

He left the bay and Erin wanted to follow him but knew she had to wait for the nurse.

Twenty minutes later, Erin emerged from her cubicle, her arm braced in a sling. She found Tate at the other end of the emergency room bay. He was awake.

"What happened, Sis? All I remember is my horse rearing, then nothing?"

"Your horse rolled over and threw you off. Sawyer and I got you back on your horse, but then Sawyer got knocked out."

Her brother looked at her arm. She started to shrug, but the pain stopped her. "I don't know what hit me, but I got a whopper of a bruise."

"Are you okay?" he asked.

"Nothing's broken." She carefully studied her brother. "And you?"

"My forearm's broken, and I have a couple of cracked ribs. I don't have a concussion, but I do have a massive headache. I think I can go home today, but the doc thinks I should stay the night." Tate waved his arms. "He said something about us being out in the middle of nowhere and if I needed help it was better to be here for twenty-four hours."

"He's right. Besides, Mom would like you and Dad here so she can keep an eye on both of you."

Tate considered her words. "I guess you're right. Have you seen Sawyer?"

"Now that I know you're okay, I'm going to go find him."

Tate started to get up, but she gently touched his shoulder. "Wait for Mom."

Nodding, he lay back down.

At the nurses' station Erin found the doctor who had treated her. "Where's the other man who was brought in with us?"

"Are you his wife?" the doctor asked.

"No."

"Are you related to him in any way?"

"Work colleagues."

"Do you know if he has any family close that we can contact in this emergency?"

Erin's heart raced. What was wrong with Sawyer? "No. I know he has a brother, but I don't know his name or number. Wasn't his cell phone on him when they brought him in?"

The doctor turned to the nurse and asked her to find out if there was a cell phone in Sawyer's belongings.

Erin walked out of the ER and ran into Sylvia.

"What happened?" Sylvia asked, observing Erin's condition.

Erin rubbed her hand over her face. "There was a riding accident this afternoon with my brother, Sawyer and me. My brother's going to be okay, but Sawyer—"

Sylvia paled and stumbled toward the nurses'

station inside the ER. "What's wrong with him?" she whispered.

"The doctor won't tell me what's wrong and needs to contact his family. I know he had his cell phone when we started the ride, but it wasn't in the helicopter when they brought him into the emergency room. We're looking for his brother."

The doctor saw Erin. "Did you find a relative?"

Sylvia spoke first. "I'm Sawyer's mother, and you can talk to me. I can give you any permission you need. I know his birth date and know what medications he's allergic to. What is his condition?"

Erin's mouth dropped open. "Surely—"

"It's a long story, Erin, but Sawyer's my son and I can give permission for treatment. I assume he isn't married."

Erin nodded.

After consulting with the doctor and signing the papers, Sylvia came back to Erin and sat down.

Erin studied the woman. "You're nothing like Sawyer described."

A sad smile curved Sylvia's mouth. "That woman's dead."

Chapter Twelve

Sylvia sat beside Erin in the chairs just inside the emergency room doors. "I'm ashamed of what kind of mother I was." She looked down at her hands. "That woman is dead."

Sylvia remained quiet for a long time.

"You don't have to tell me about it," Erin reassured her.

She shook her head. "Has Sawyer mentioned me?"

"Yes. I was complaining about my mother and he tried to reassure me—"

Sylvia's shook her head. "Surely, not your mother. She's been wonderful since your dad was brought in. She's been a rock for all of the other women who've had their husbands on the floor."

"What I've learned is that we all have feet of clay."

"That's hard to believe."

"It's true, as both Mom and I have discovered."

With her hands clasped tightly in her lap, Sylvia began. "The wheels came off our life after my husband died of a heart attack. I was lost. I depended on him for everything. Neither of us had parents. We knew each other from foster care. Two lonely souls were attracted to each other. We weren't in love, but married, just to have someone. Once Dennis died, there was no one except my two teenage sons. Left alone with the responsibility for them, I panicked, and my boys suffered." She closed her eyes and took a deep breath. "What I would give if I could go back and change what I did. But I can't."

Sylvia explained what happened next with her series of boyfriends. "When you're in a program like AA, you learn to accept responsibility for your actions. It was my fault. I brought those men into our home. I don't blame Caleb or Sawyer. The best thing Caleb did was leave and take his brother with him."

Erin laid her hand over Sylvia's and squeezed. "He's an amazing man. I hate to admit it, but I'm glad he won the contract over me. He recognized things in my brother that never would've occurred to me, but once I knew there was a problem, I could do something about it."

"Where are they?" Mary Morning Star demanded.

"They are here, Sister," Betty said, holding Mary's arm.

"There you are, Daughter." Mary hurried across the room. Looking at Erin's sling, Mary stopped short.

"I've only got a bruised arm and my shoulder was dislocated. They put it back into place. It's sore, but I'll be okay." Erin stood.

Mary looked at Sylvia for a confirmation.

"That's true."

Tenderly, Mary wrapped her arms around her daughter and held her.

Betty stepped forward. "I thought your mom was going to pass out on me, too, when you went down." She explained how they'd waited for the helicopter, loaded in the three patients and then taken off.

"I don't believe your mother ever went the speed limit on our drive here," Betty added.

"How are your brother and Sawyer?" Mary asked.

"Tate's fine. They cast his arm and want to keep him for the night for observation. But Sawyer hasn't regained consciousness. They want to run some other tests."

"Do we need to contact someone in his family to give permission?"

"No need," Sylvia spoke. "I gave it."

Mary and Betty stared at her. "I thought only relatives could give permission," Mary said.

"That's right. I'm Sawyer's mother."

Betty's jaw dropped and Mary gaped.

"How?" Mary asked.

"There's time for that later, Mom. Why don't you go and find Tate? I believe he wants to see you. Now, he would not admit it, being a boy his age, but he needs you, just like I need you."

Mary grabbed Erin's free hand and held it to her chest, then leaned down and kissed her. "Thank you for bringing your brother home. And how you managed to bring in two men and three horses, I'll never know, but I'm proud of you, Daughter."

After a moment, Mary and Betty headed off. At the door, Betty stopped and held up something in her hand. "Here's Sawyer's phone. We found it on the floor of the barn after the paramedics took the three of you off in the helicopter. I thought you might need it to contact Sawyer's relatives. Of course, you don't need it now, but why don't you keep it for him? You know how I am with this stuff." Betty gave the phone to Erin, then followed Mary.

Erin stared down at the fancy phone.

"He's come a long way since he was a teenager who was always begging for a fight," Sylvia whispered.

"Have you ever thought that he might've been trying to protect his mother?"

Sylvia's face lost all color.

The moment the words popped out of Erin's

mouth, she knew she'd made a mistake. "I'm sorry, Sylvia."

"That's okay. You were only telling the truth." Unsteadily she rose to her feet. "I arrived early for my shift, but now I've got to get to work. See you later."

Erin felt as if she'd just crawled out from underneath a rock. She tried to access Sawyer's phone but didn't know the password. She thought and thought, wondering what he would use. What was his horse's name?

Suddenly the phone sprang to life. A name appeared on the screen: Caleb Jensen, Sawyer's brother.

"Hello."

The other end remained quiet.

"Caleb?"

"Yes and who are you?"

The man didn't sound welcoming. "I'm Erin Delong, and I'm glad you called."

"Why is that?" He didn't seem too pleased that she had answered Sawyer's phone.

"There's been an accident. I needed to get a hold of you so you could give the doctors permission to treat Sawyer for his injuries, but apparently, your mother works at this hospital and gave her permission."

"I don't know what joke you're trying to play, but it isn't funny." The tone of Caleb's voice let her know he didn't appreciate any foolishness.

"It's not a joke," Erin reassured him. "Sawyer, my brother and I were caught in a freak storm out on the range behind our ranch house, and we all ended up in Albuquerque at the University Hospital. You might want to come see him, and your mother."

"There's been a lot of miracles in the history of the world, but, lady, I don't appreciate you including my mother in that group. Why don't you give the doctors my number, and I'll talk to them."

"Then give me your number because I'll never get into this phone again."

Caleb told her his number and hung up. The man didn't sound happy, but knowing what she did about the boys' upbringing, Erin couldn't hold it against him. She found the doctor and gave him Caleb's number. The room swirled around her and she stumbled into the doctor.

"If you don't sit down, lady, you're going to end up in a bed next to your brother."

Erin knew he was right and walked to the waiting room at the end of the hall and sat. She laid her head back against the couch and prayed.

It was going to be a long, difficult night.

Finally, after several visits to her brother's and father's rooms, Erin ended up in Sawyer's room. Her mother stayed with her father, and Betty settled in with Tate.

Slowly, Erin walked to the bed. Sawyer still

hadn't awakened. "This isn't exactly the way I thought we'd wind up. It was just supposed to be a ride, Sawyer, not some life-changing event." Picking up his hand, she held it to her cheek. "C'mon, Sawyer, wake up. I need to see your eyes. So much has happened that you'd love to know.

"You might've been unconscious, but you did a great job riding in, staying in the saddle. If there was any doubt about you being a cowboy, it's gone. And if you hadn't been there, I never would've gotten my brother onto his horse." She didn't mention the bruise she sported when round two of the wind struck. "You'll have to put that on your résumé—the man can stay on a horse even if he's unconscious."

"That's an impressive thing to put on one's résumé," said an unknown voice.

Erin looked over her shoulder and saw an older version of Sawyer. "You must be Caleb."

He nodded, stepping next to her. He pointedly looked at her clutching Sawyer's hand. "How's he doing?"

She didn't want to let go of Sawyer, but at the steely look from his brother, she released Sawyer's hand, gently placing it on the bed. "The doctors say he's doing fine, but for some reason, he hasn't woken up." Her voice got thick and she struggled.

Caleb studied his brother. "He was always the one to stir things up."

"I know. He told me he was always in trouble."

Caleb's eyes narrowed. "I'm surprised he said anything at all."

"He tried to encourage me when I got all wobbly about my mother."

"Oh?"

The word hung in the air.

"He saw something I didn't and inconveniently pointed it out."

Caleb smiled. "That sounds like my brother. He's got a talent."

"True, but the way he said it lessened the blow." She stared down into Sawyer's sleeping face. She wanted to run her fingers over his cheek but didn't think his brother would appreciate the action. "Was he always like that?" Looking up, she caught Caleb's look of surprise. He quickly masked it.

"He's had his moments."

What did that mean? "I've been impressed with Sawyer's ability to bring the town folks in. And, he's listened to suggestions."

"That's part of his job."

She found herself lovingly studying Sawyer. His beard showed, making it look as if he'd just ridden in from the range, and his brown hair could use a good cut. She pushed a lock back from his forehead, unable to hold back from touching him.

Tears welled in her eyes as she remembered how he'd reached out to her and Tate without any hesitation. "No, what he's done for my family is more than just making the rodeo redo go smoothly." Looking up, she didn't hide what was in her heart.

Caleb swallowed. "You said something about my mother."

Erin stepped away from the bed. Of course, Caleb would want to know about his mother. "Sylvia's the night nurse on the floor above us where my father is. We met her when Dad was hospitalized for a stroke.

"When the helicopter brought us in earlier today, the doctors wanted a contact number for Sawyer. I told Sylvia, and that's when she revealed she was Sawyer's mom. He saw her yesterday when he came with me to see my dad."

The world clicked in place and she understood Sawyer's silence driving home last night. He'd come face-to-face with his mother. The mother who'd abandoned him, who'd sided with temporary boyfriends over her own sons. He'd been wrestling with the ugliness of his past.

"So, how'd you come by my brother's phone?"

Caleb's clipped tone snapped her out of the memory. "When my mother and aunt drove in from Tucumcari, they brought his phone with them since it had fallen out of his pocket when we pulled him off my dad's horse. That's why I had it when you called. Would you like for me to get your mother? I'm sure she could take a break."

Caleb shook his head. "There'll be enough time to talk to her later."

The tone of his voice said he was done talking about his mother and he didn't want to talk to her, either. But Caleb Jensen didn't know Erin wasn't one to back down. She wanted to stay with Sawyer a little bit longer.

"Do you plan to stay in Albuquerque for long? I think the hospital will allow you to bunk in here, but you probably need to check with the nurses to make sure it's okay."

He folded his arms across his chest and took on a steely look. "I don't plan on leaving my brother, so I guess I'll need to talk to his doctor."

"Check with the nurses' station just outside. They'll have the doctor's name and how to get in contact with him." Erin didn't move.

Caleb nodded and left.

She turned back to Sawyer, picking up his hand, again. "I hope you don't mind I ran your brother off, but he was trying to intimidate me. And he didn't want to talk to your mother, either." She stroked the back of her fingers across his cheek. "You need to wake up. I now know why you were so quiet last night and today before all of this happened, but you don't know this new woman your mom's become. She's nothing like the woman you told me about. Please open those beautiful hazel eyes."

She heard a commotion out in the hall. Rushing from the room, Erin saw Caleb facing Sylvia. From their body language, the confrontation wasn't going well.

"What right do you have to assume any medical decisions for Sawyer? You haven't been in our lives for the last fifteen years, so what makes you think you're allowed to make decisions now?"

Sylvia blanched as if her son hit her.

Erin moved to her side. "This isn't the time or the place for this discussion. Besides, Sylvia was the only one here when the doctors needed permission." She looked from mother to son. "Would you rather have had Sawyer not treated? What if there'd been a brain bleed? Would you have wanted them to waste time trying to contact you and not treat your brother?"

Caleb took a step back as if her words nearly flattened him. "I don't believe you. In emergency situations, doctors act all the time," he shot back.

"True," Sylvia answered, "but I was here. I told the doctors I was his mother, and maybe those extra few minutes made the difference. I don't know."

"Yeah, if that's true, why isn't he waking up?" Caleb snapped.

Sylvia's shoulders hunched, and her eyes filled with moisture. "I don't know," she whispered.

Erin glared daggers at Caleb, slipped her arm around Sylvia's shoulders and led her to the elevators. Nothing was said while they waited, but Erin felt the woman's pain.

Once they were inside the elevator car, Erin said, "He's speaking out of hurt and fear."

"I know, but what he's saying is true." Her stark words only reinforced the somberness of the situation.

When the doors slid open, Sylvia walked off. Erin looked down at her watch and realized that Sylvia still had time on her shift. Erin went to her father's room. Both of her parents were sleeping, and Erin slumped down into the single chair.

She tried to take in what had just happened. She didn't blame Caleb and Sawyer for their feelings about their mother and what had happened, but her sons needed to become acquainted with the woman their mother was now before they made any judgments.

"Oh, Lord, help us to deal with the situations we find ourselves in."

Voices drew Sawyer from his sleep. He recognized one voice, Caleb's, but not the other.

"I'm sorry, Son. There was no excuse. Forgive me."

"That's easy to say now," he said, "but it doesn't change the past."

"I know…"

The conversation slipped beneath the surface of sleep. When Sawyer next woke up, darkness surrounded him except for the night-light by the sink. He remained still for a moment, cataloging the sounds he heard. A cart with a wobbly wheel went by his room; he noted voices in the distance as people walked by. The smell of antiseptic filled his nostrils. He cast his mind back, trying to remember what had happened. Obviously, he was in the hospital, but how had he gotten here? What day was it?

The last thing he remembered was the sand-and windstorm. He'd just put Tate on his horse, mounted his own, then—nothing. When did it happen? Why was he in the hospital? He ran his fingers through his hair and felt the bump. He jerked his hand away from his head. He had quite a lump.

Obviously, they'd gotten Tate help, but there was a whole lot of memory missing.

The door to his room opened. Outlined in the light from the hall was a woman, and from her shape he knew it wasn't Erin. The woman stepped into the room and allowed the door to slowly close.

"You're awake."

His mother.

"How are you feeling?" She stepped closer so he could see her face in the light from the night-light in the room.

"Like I've been kicked by a bull."

"I'll tell the nurse you're awake." She disappeared. Several minutes later, she and the floor nurse walked in.

"Welcome back to the world, Mr. Jensen. I'll call and let the doctor know you're awake. You gave us quite a scare there." Before she left the room, she took Sawyer's vitals, wrote them down and patted his mother on the shoulder. "You must be excited your son's finally awake after two days."

"I am. It's an answer to prayer." Sylvia nodded. Once they were alone, she moved to the side of his bed but remained quiet for a long time.

Sawyer still didn't know what to think. He often wondered if his mom was still alive, but he never imagined her like this.

"I know you have a million questions, but I'd like to tell you what happened if you'd let me. If you don't, I'll walk out of this room and not bother you." She stood by the door waiting for his answer.

He didn't know what to think. Was this reality? Maybe he had had a psychotic break.

The floor nurse came in. "I called the doctor. The resident should be in within a few moments, and the doctor should be by tomorrow morning, first thing."

For the next twenty minutes he was poked and prodded.

When he looked around again, his mother had disappeared. That psychotic-break thing was looking better and better.

When he woke again, the room was still dark, but he saw a figure by the door.

She walked to his bed. Her hand shook as she crossed her arms across her chest and tucked her hands under her arms.

"I thought you'd skipped out on me again." He sounded like an eight-year-old boy.

"I'm still on duty on the floor above. This is my break."

The reason rang true.

"I wanted to try to explain some things to you."

As if that was possible, Sawyer thought, but he said nothing.

"After Caleb won his emancipation and took you away, my boyfriend left, blaming me that we couldn't get more money from you. I was alone. At thirty-five, I didn't know how to take care of myself." She paused, lost in some memory.

"I ran through a series of boyfriends who beat me and used me. My last boyfriend, before I got sober, beat me up badly and left me on the side of the road. I probably would've died if Neil Turner hadn't found me and taken me to the clinic that he runs here in Albuquerque. Neil is also a recovering drug user, and he recognized a woman at the end of her rope. It took me months to recover, but, fortunately, Neil's clinic had places for homeless and abused women like me. The people there encouraged me to go to AA. Neil took me to their meetings. He helped me find a job, an apartment and encouraged me to go back to school.

"Neil also took me back to church. I've been sober nine years, eight months and eleven days."

If he wasn't so angry, he might be impressed. "Did you ever try to find us, Mom?" Sawyer bit out. "Did you ever wonder about us? Ever give a rat's rear if Caleb and I were alive or dead?" He heard the harsh words coming out of his mouth but couldn't control them. They spilled out with a raging hurt he didn't realize was still inside him.

She flinched as if he struck her. "I wasn't sober most of those years, but the times I was, and remembered my sons, I wanted another drink or hit off a joint to drown my guilt."

She looked down at her hands. "I didn't want to remember the terrible things I'd done." Taking another deep breath, she continued. "I remember siding with my boyfriends against my sons. Allowing you to be beaten, and then blaming it on you.

"It's an ache in my heart that doesn't go away.

Lately, I've wanted to hire a detective to find you and Caleb, but I hadn't worked up the courage. Forgive me, Sawyer."

In the shadows, he couldn't see her eyes, but he heard the pain in her voice. She waited.

"I don't know, Mom. Caleb and I lived too long supporting ourselves and only depending on each other. It's a lot to think about."

"I can't ask for anything more." She touched his arm. "Thank you. I have to go back to work." With those words she turned and left.

Light spilled into the room, then, as the door drifted closed, the light winked out.

Staring at the ceiling, Sawyer had never imagined how his life would change this day. It should've come with a neon sign warning Danger Ahead. Instead, it came with him oversleeping for church and riding out with an amazing woman.

He'd often wondered if his mother was still alive. Caleb never mentioned her, but Sawyer often thought of her. Even as a teen, something inside him thought that if his mom ever got her life together, she'd be an amazing person. Before their dad had died, they could depend upon her. She'd embraced her family, made a home, but once they buried Dad and were thrown off the ranch, she'd unraveled quickly. From the looks of things now, it seemed she had gotten her life back together.

She'd been going to AA. And caring for Erin's dad. Erin and Mary loved her. That he didn't understand.

Could he turn his back on his mom, ignore her? How could he forgive what she'd done? He remembered all the beatings he got, sticking up for her and then her siding with her boyfriends.

When he told Erin of that last beating he got, the memory seared his soul as if it happened yesterday. Sawyer remembered their mother yelling at Caleb to stop hitting her boyfriend. Caleb shook her off, pulled Sawyer to his feet, and the two boys ran out into the backyard. They'd slipped through the side gate and Caleb dragged Sawyer forward. When Caleb started to run, Sawyer fell. Caleb picked him up, slipped his arm around Sawyer's chest and half walked and carried him to the far side of the field behind their house.

When Sawyer's nose wouldn't stop bleeding, they walked to the clinic the next street over. They didn't dare go to a hospital emergency room because the authorities would want to know where their parents were. The clinic dealt with street kids and wasn't as strict. They treated first, then asked questions. Neither boy wanted to rat their mother out.

They'd taped up Sawyer's nose and made sure nothing else was broken. When it came time to pay, Caleb wrote an IOU and they'd slipped out the back door. Oddly enough, the boys had paid every cent of that clinic bill. It might've taken two years, but they'd paid in full.

After that incident, Caleb and Sawyer spent as little time as they could at the house. That incident had been the last straw for the boys. Caleb knew Sawyer couldn't take another beating like that. Often, they slept over with their friends. The father of one of Caleb's friends was a lawyer and helped Caleb file for his emancipation. Once granted, Sawyer lived with his brother.

Their mother visited them once when her boyfriend beat her up. She wanted money from them. They gave it to her, but the boys left the next week since school ended. That was the last time they'd seen their mother.

Sawyer closed his eyes. He knew his mother didn't remember half the things that had happened. Now that she was clean and sober, she wanted forgiveness. She had no idea of most of what she wanted forgiveness for. Could he do that?

He didn't know.

As he thought about the last few days, he still couldn't take in what Erin had done on Sunday. What had started as an afternoon ride where he'd hoped to talk to Tate had turned into a nightmare. From what he could recall, none of them should've survived that storm, and yet, obviously Erin had brought both him and Tate home.

Amazing.

She awed him. He lo—

His head hurt and he turned his head on the pillow, not wanting to think about it anymore.

Chapter Thirteen

Early the next morning, Caleb walked into Sawyer's room. He moved quietly.

"What are you doing here?" Sawyer asked.

Caleb jerked toward the sound of Sawyer's voice. He took several steps toward the head of the bed. "It's been three days since they brought you in. Folks were worried. Little did I know what a stinking attitude you'd have when you woke. It's a good thing I left my wife at home, because she could've given you a run for your money."

Three days? "Really?"

Caleb stopped. "Yeah."

Sawyer heard a wealth of meaning in that sound. But he noted something else in his voice. He grinned. "Is the morning sickness any better?" he asked.

"No."

"So, how did you know about what happened?" Sawyer asked.

"I called your phone, got Erin and she told me what happened to you. But then she continued on with an amazing story, which I found hard to believe."

Leaning back, Sawyer closed his eyes, as shocked by the story as Caleb. "Believe it. Mom's alive and working in this hospital. She's one of the floor nurses on the next floor up, where Erin's father is."

Caleb sat in the chair next to the bed. "If you'd told me you were attacked by little green men from Mars, I'd find that easier to believe."

"You're not the only one. I thought I was hallucinating when she walked into Detrick's hospital room as the nurse, but I wasn't. It creeped me out. There, standing before me, was a nurse who looked like our mom, sounded like her, but was a totally different creature from the one we ran away from.

"She wanted to apologize for her actions." The words had to sink in again. Sawyer still doubted what was going on. "How can you make right all the stuff that happened to us?"

Caleb studied his boot. "You think she means it?"

"I don't know. I'm living in this weird dream where I don't know anything for sure."

"So, how'd you end up here?" Caleb asked.

"Got clobbered in the head with something,

probably a branch, during a windstorm on Sunday. Can't say, since the lights went out."

Caleb smiled. "I know. Apparently, your competition for this job brought you and her brother in through that rainstorm. She got hurt herself."

Sawyer considered his brother's words. "How do you know?"

Caleb sat in the chair. "I have a story to tell you and it's a whopper."

Erin walked into Sawyer's room a little after eight in the morning. She'd spent the night in one of the rooms on the top floor of the hospital reserved for family. Both Tate and she'd been released yesterday, but her father had had a complication. He'd suffered another smaller stroke, and the surgeons were debating if he should be taken into surgery. Sitting in the bed, Sawyer had his breakfast tray in front of him. Caleb sat beside the bed.

"You're awake." Relief washed through her. She'd prayed for Sawyer and her dad through the night. Every time the worst-case scenario popped into her head, she pushed it out. They would be okay. Crossing to the bed, she stopped herself from kissing Sawyer. "When you didn't wake—" She took a deep breath.

"He's been known to be contrary," Caleb offered.

He wasn't the only one, Erin thought. "I can believe that." She followed her words with a smile.

"In the middle of the night, my eyes popped open. It was a relief to see Caleb walking in here this morning. He said he'd talked to you on the phone."

"That's true. Mom and Aunt Betty brought your phone. Before I could figure how to unlock it to notify your brother, he called."

"Yes, Caleb told me." He looked at her sling. "I don't remember you getting hurt."

"There's a lot you don't know about Sunday. But, as I told your brother, you could put on your résumé—can ride while unconscious. I was impressed and grateful."

He nodded toward her arm. "So what happened to you?"

"The wind not only picked up the branch that knocked you out, it hit me in the back with something that made me see stars. A bad bruise to my clavicle, so I guess I can put on my résumé—isn't easily knocked off her horse." He didn't know the sheer terror that had coursed through her that day, and she wouldn't admit it.

The door opened. Mary, Betty and Tate walked in.

"Tate wanted to check on you before he left and went home," Mary explained.

"So how are you, Tate?" Sawyer asked.

"I'm okay. They checked me out and think hitting the ground the way I did is the cause of why I passed out." Tate shrugged.

"That's not uncommon. Both Erin and I worried that your horse had rolled over on you. We couldn't tell."

"How long you going to be here?" Tate asked. "Are they going to let you go today?"

"I haven't seen the doctor yet, but I feel fine. Ready to go. And if I get sprung today, Caleb will drive me to your ranch to pick up my truck."

With a round of final goodbyes, the group left. Mary looked at Erin. "We'll give you a few seconds."

Erin nodded. She moved to the bed and stood by Sawyer's head.

"I'll be outside if you need anything, Sawyer." Caleb left the room.

Once alone, she smiled at him. "I don't think your brother was too thrilled with me. When I talked to him on the phone, he wasn't impressed."

"He's protective of me."

"I know."

"And you've talked to your mother?"

His face froze and the curtain of his eyes closed. "Yes, I've talked to her."

"I knew Sylvia as my father's nurse. She helped Mom, talked to her when we were sick with worry, answered our questions and arranged for Mom to stay in one of the guest rooms on the top floor. When my sister, Kai, would drive over from her apartment, she always had Sylvia update her on Dad's condition. Kai thinks your mom is super. We could ask her any question and she'd answer it."

She wrapped her hand around his and squeezed.

Erin continued. "I think what you and your brother did to survive and do well is amazing, and I admire both of you for doing it. But you've got a second chance with your mom. Don't throw it away. The person she is now is amazing."

"You didn't live through our hell."

"True, but I know that you need to give your mom a chance."

"And have you forgiven your father?"

Ah, he took no hostages. "I did. We talked, and I think that God sent you here to do more than work on a rodeo. Maybe you were here to minister to each member of my family. And, maybe you're ready and your mom's ready to heal the wounds of the past."

He pulled his hand out of hers.

"I'm going back with Betty and Tate. Someone needs to be there to take care of the rodeo redo. If we're going to get things finished on time, we need to make some decisions."

"I think I can go home today."

She felt him withdraw from her. "Let's hope so, but I'll go back now, in any case." She wanted to kiss him, but Sawyer had put up a wall and didn't seem to invite the intimacy. "Goodbye."

With each step, she felt him growing more detached, leaving a chasm between them, and the bright light of hope dimmed.

The doctor released Sawyer from the hospital, but only after he made an appointment for a follow-up visit.

"Did you talk to Mom?" Sawyer asked Caleb.

"No."

"You didn't want to talk to her?" If Sawyer had a bad reaction, Caleb's stank.

"No."

"Then, I guess you'd better not tell your wife you ran into her."

Caleb's jaw flexed.

"Your wife might want your kid to have a grandmother."

"She'll have a grandfather."

"A girl? You're going to have a girl?"

Caleb's shoulders relaxed. "Yeah, they did a lot of tests on Brenda since she had so much internal damage from the bomb blast in Iraq. We didn't think we'd be able to have kids and had decided to adopt when we discovered our wonderful news."

That wasn't the only astounding news. Their mother had been thrust into their lives again.

"So, Erin was the one you were competing against."

"What?" Caleb's question brought Sawyer out of his thoughts.

"Erin Delong, the lady I've been dealing with."

Caleb glanced at Sawyer and grinned. He turned his gaze back to the road.

"And why are you giving her such a hard time?"

"Whoa. Back it up. I call you and some strange woman answers, then tells me my mother gave permission for you to be treated. It kinda sets your world on fire."

Sawyer understood his brother's reasoning. A lot of things had happened over the past few days. He thought about the courage and grit Erin had shown with her back to the wall. Not many people could've pulled that off. "I'm still in awe of what she did. That was not an easy ride with me and her brother. She's got guts." His mind went to how she'd originally dealt with him and then worked with him on setting up things for the bids on the rodeo.

And she took advice.

"That's quite a smile. What are you thinking about?"

Sawyer turned toward his brother, since his neck was still a little stiff. "Erin and what happened on Sunday."

"What were you doing out in the middle of a storm?" Caleb frowned. "I thought you had more sense than that?"

"C'mon, Caleb, you ever get caught off guard?"

Caleb's cheek flexed.

"The afternoon started out perfect. No sign of

a cloud or any forecast of one. I'd promised Tate a ride, and the poor kid needed some time with another guy."

"So how'd the girl get involved?"

"Erin's smart and listened as her brother and I talked. When Tate ditched school one afternoon, she listened to my advice before confronting him."

Caleb threw him a grin. "I'm impressed. She wasn't the troll you first thought she'd be."

Sawyer realized that he hadn't thought of Erin in those terms in a long time. "Well, I had just finished a couple of projects that had been real headaches. I was prepared for the worst."

Caleb didn't follow up with another question, and that wasn't like him.

"What's set you off?"

His brother didn't answer, but looked back out on I-40. They were halfway between Albuquerque and Tucumcari. They had another hour or hour and half left before they got to the Delong ranch.

Sighing, Caleb shook his head. "I didn't tell Brenda about Mom being with you. I didn't want to argue with her about the situation, but somehow or some way she'll find out. It's scary how she does that, but she'll discover it. I'm wondering when to tell her."

"The sooner the better," Sawyer added.

"Hey, buddy, you're in the same spot as me.

I didn't see you embrace Mom and tell her all's well." The harshness of Caleb's voice took Sawyer aback.

"I'd just come back to my senses. You were awake the entire time." Sawyer stared at his brother. "Wait, how did you know Mom slipped into my room?"

"I got to the hospital long before you regained consciousness. I'd walked out of your room that night to get some coffee, when I saw Mom slip into your room. I stood outside the door and listened as she talked to you. When she came out and saw me, she opened her mouth, but I shook my head. I heard your response to her explanation."

A vague memory of Caleb arguing with someone floated through his brain. "So what if I snarled? You haven't done so hot yourself."

This was the first time Sawyer could remember them arguing. They'd been a team for as long as he could remember. That's how they survived. Now…

"We might call Pastor Garvey in Plainview and talk to him. And you could tell him about your becoming a father."

Caleb's hands opened out from the steering wheel and then regripped it. "We sound like we're fourteen and sixteen again."

"That's probably because we feel that way."

Sawyer shook his head. "Who would've

thought?" But that's what they were going to do, talk to their pastor. Too bad he couldn't talk to his brother as easily as he talked to Erin when they'd gone to Las Vegas and Albuquerque. Of course, she'd turned his words back on him, so maybe he didn't need to talk to her. But if he couldn't get past this obstacle, would he lose Erin?

When Sawyer and Caleb pulled into the ranch driveway, the Delongs had just sat down for dinner. Tate jumped up and urged the men to join them. Sawyer had no more success refusing Mary's invitation than he had last week.

No one said anything about Sylvia, but she could've been at the table.

"So you're going back to school tomorrow, Tate?" Sawyer asked.

"I am and will have lots of makeup work to do."

"I don't doubt you will catch up," Sawyer reassured him.

"Sawyer tells me that you were a pickup rider in the rodeo," Tate said.

Caleb nodded. "I was, but I like staying in one place for more than a week."

"You don't miss the traveling?" Tate asked.

Erin tensed. What was going on with her brother? He kept saying he hated rodeo, but now suddenly he was asking questions about the professional circuit.

"No, I don't miss it. I'll say rodeo helped Sawyer and I support ourselves, but if we'd been given a choice, we probably wouldn't have gone that route."

Erin knew every word Caleb spoke was the truth, but you had to love your sport to put up with the traveling and never settling down.

After the meal, Erin moved to Caleb's side. "Thanks for answering Tate's questions. I put myself through graduate school like Sawyer with my barrel-racing winnings, but hearing it from a male's perspective made the statements valid."

"Not a problem. Rodeo saved both Sawyer and me."

"I know."

Caleb glanced at his brother, who was talking to Mary and Tate. "He told you?"

"He did. He wanted to show me that my mother's actions were mild and could be worked out, as compared to the problems you two had with your mom."

Caleb studied his brother.

"He was right, but he needs to follow his own advice."

Sawyer's words hit home, and Caleb snapped upright.

"I guess he's not the only one," she added.

Fire ignited in Caleb's eyes. "You don't know what you're talking about."

"Maybe, but I haven't read an exception in the

Bible that Caleb and Sawyer Jensen get a waiver when it comes to forgiveness."

Caleb opened his mouth, then clamped it shut. "Sawyer, I'm leaving."

Immediately he joined his brother. "You're not going to drive home to Peaster tonight, are you? That's more than a seven-hour drive."

"I'd planned on it. I've done harder drives with no problems."

Sawyer stepped closer to his brother and whispered something. Caleb gave a single nod, then walked outside.

"Thanks for the meal, ladies." Sawyer followed his words with a smile. "I'll see you tomorrow."

Turning to Erin, he nodded to her and started outside.

"Sawyer," Erin called.

He stopped and turned. The closed expression on his face didn't encourage talk.

Her heart ached. "Remember what we talked about Saturday afternoon. You were right on target."

"If my mom would've been as good as your mom, it wouldn't be a problem."

"So your advice only works if the problem's someone else's?"

The muscles in his jaw flexed, and his gaze narrowed. She could see all sorts of emotions racing through his eyes. Finally, he turned and walked out of the house without giving her the courtesy of a response.

She wanted to rush after him and scream and stomp her foot. He willingly gave advice but, apparently, couldn't take it. She didn't know how their relationship would work if he could only give advice and not follow it.

But, inside, she knew that wasn't true. He'd listened before, but why not now?

Sawyer grabbed his cell phone and dialed Pastor Garvey's number, putting it in speaker mode. Caleb sat in the chair beside the table in his motel room and glared at him. Pastor picked up on the first ring. Sawyer quickly identified himself. After a couple of minutes of polite talk, the pastor said, "It's good to hear from you, Sawyer, but I think there's another reason for your call."

"You were always good about reading me."

"I'm glad to hear from the Jensen brothers, but you don't often call to talk."

Sawyer looked into his brother's eyes. "We ran into our mother the other day."

The other end of the line remained quiet.

"I was hurt and taken to a hospital in Albuquerque," Sawyer explained. "Mom works there as a floor nurse. She's clean and sober and claims to be a Christian."

"That's good news. I know y'all never thought to see her again."

"She's in AA and church, Pastor."

"But she asked for our forgiveness," Caleb blurted out.

Sawyer, who sat on the corner of the bed, stared at his brother, surprised he'd revealed that.

"And you're not willing to do that?" Pastor Garvey replied.

"No." Caleb's hands fisted.

During the entire time Caleb had been Sawyer's guardian, he'd never mentioned their mother, which was why his brother's reaction now flabbergasted Sawyer.

"She's only asking for forgiveness, Caleb. Not absolution. There's a difference."

Caleb lurched to his feet and walked out of the room, slamming the door behind him.

"I guess my explanation didn't go over too well," Pastor Garvey said.

"His reaction has surprised me, but I'm having a hard time with it, too. How can we just forget how she wronged us?"

"Grace, Sawyer. Let God work in your heart and quit worrying how you can forgive her. Just do it. It's a decision, not a feeling. Choose to do it."

"Thanks, Pastor." Sawyer looked down at his phone. Was it that easy?

No, doing what Pastor said wouldn't be easy. Of course, he'd advised Erin to do that very same thing with her parents. Had she done it? He didn't know, but their offenses didn't come anywhere close to his mother's.

But was there a measure of grace, a point where you stop forgiving? Jesus said to forgive seventy times seven.

Forgiveness?

He struggled with that question all night.

Chapter Fourteen

Sawyer and Caleb walked to Lulu's for breakfast. Sawyer had managed to convince his brother to spend the night by pointing out that Caleb now had a wife and child depending on him, and Caleb needed not to take risks, such as leaving Tucumcari at ten thirty at night. That did the trick.

"Lulu will feed you any meal you need," Sawyer told his brother.

Entering the restaurant, several people called out a welcome to Sawyer. He introduced his brother with pride to the residents, talked about his adventure in Albuquerque and the helicopter ride.

"I hear it was our Erin who hauled you all in," Bob Rivera said. He introduced the men with him, salesmen who made their monthly trip out to this part of New Mexico.

"It was her, indeed."

"That's not unusual for our Erin," Bob explained to the men at the table. "I remember one time when my daughter drove to Las Vegas. She blew two tires and ended up in a ditch. The cell reception in that area of the state is spotty, at best, and my daughter couldn't dial for help. Erin drove by, took her into Vegas, and then drove her back to her car to make sure the tow truck got it right. Erin picks up any challenge thrown at her."

It took several more minutes before they got up to the order counter. After ordering, they grabbed empty cups and walked to the coffee urn in the corner of the room. With Lulu's daughter away on a school trip, it was every man for himself, but Lulu's cooking made it worth it.

They settled at a table in the corner. Caleb looked around. "Looks like you found a home, with all the greetings called out to you."

Sawyer sat up straighter and thought about it. He'd felt at ease ever since he drove into this town. "Could be. Was it like that when you first went to the Kaye place?"

Caleb played with the handle of his coffee mug. "It was, and with each visit, I settled in more and more. I allowed myself to let down my guard. After the accident, the Kaye ranch became my refuge."

When one of the cowboys Caleb helped as a pickup rider in the ring got hurt, Caleb nearly folded with guilt and retreated to his friend's ranch. Sawyer had worried his brother wouldn't recover from the incident.

"The minute Brenda showed up, well, I knew she would have a major effect on my life."

Sawyer laughed. "Having met your wife, I knew she'd have an effect, too."

Caleb took a sip of his coffee. "So have you run across *your* Brenda?"

"Sawyer, your breakfast's up," Lulu called out. They retrieved their meals and began to eat.

"Are you going to answer my question? I remember you pressing me hard about my wife."

Sawyer recalled the night they'd spent in the small living compartment of Caleb's horse trailer, talking. "Well, I've never met someone like Erin. I thought she would be a headache for me while I worked on this project, but she's helped.

"It was her idea to post the jobs for the locals, and in the future, as I do other projects, I'll work it the same way as this one."

"The website is a great idea," Caleb said.

"Well, that came from another local, but without Erin pushing, it wouldn't have happened." He leaned in. "It's a weird experience to argue with her, because she argues back and meets my arguments with her own. She thinks and can be reasoned with, and I can change her mind." He shook his head.

Caleb grinned. "Did it throw you off your stride? Make you wonder what was happening?"

"It did. She's a strong woman, so unlike—" He clamped down on the word, not wanting to mention their mother. They purposely hadn't discussed their mother after they'd talked to Pastor Garvey, but they needed to. She was the elephant in the room.

Sawyer sat back and took a sip of coffee, determined to clear the air. "You know we're both going to have to deal with it."

Caleb stared down at the table. "I hear ya."

"And what? Did you talk to Mom?"

"No."

"Why not?" Sawyer pressed. He felt like a hypocrite, unable to do it himself, but things needed to be said.

"Why am I suddenly the bad guy here? How crazy is that?" Caleb demanded.

"Since you're going to be a daddy, you need to deal with some of the garbage we went through. Garbage left in our lives and stuff you don't want to pass on to that new baby."

"I'm not the only one. Have you forgiven Mom?" Caleb didn't pull any punches.

"No, but I need to."

Rubbing the back of his neck, Caleb sighed. "I need the time and space, Sawyer, to think it through."

"I hear you."

It wasn't until they stood outside by Caleb's truck that Sawyer brought up their mother, again.

"I think if you talk to your wife about Mom, she might help."

"That's a frightening idea."

They patted each other on the back, then Caleb hopped in his truck and drove off.

It would be a struggle for the brothers to forgive, but Sawyer knew he had to. Was it as simple as Pastor Garvey said last night? Just do it? Surely not.

But when had Pastor Garvey ever steered him wrong?

Fifteen minutes later, Sawyer walked into the rodeo office. He arrived first, started coffee and sat in the boardroom with the contracts. Working his way through them, a hundred different thoughts bombarded him. He needed to get things going to meet his deadline.

The front door opened, and Lisa called out and joined him in the conference room. "I'm so glad to see you. When I heard about your accident, well, it shook me to my core. You, Tate and Erin. All three of you, and when the helicopter flew in—" She shook her head. "Folks met at church and prayed together. Then when you didn't wake up immediately, panic raced through this town. Bob kept us updated. The man hasn't ever seen so much business."

That sense of home embraced Sawyer again.

"Your prayers mean a lot to me. Thanks."

"That's what neighbors and friends do, hold up each other in prayer in times of crisis." She walked back to her desk.

Moments later, he heard the front door open again and Lisa squealed. "Oh, Erin." He heard talking and crying. Curious, he stood and investigated. Erin and Lisa stood by her desk hugging.

His eyes drank in the sight of Erin. What an amazing woman. He'd been a jerk at the hospital, he admitted to himself, cutting himself off from her, but after what had happened, he still didn't have his bearings and couldn't risk—what? His heart? His pride? And he'd just admitted he wanted to talk to her.

Finally, Erin noticed him and stepped back from Lisa. He noticed a tenseness in her body that he hadn't seen since she'd walked into the conference room that first day. She still had on her sling. "I'm a little late for work today, but it's not due to having to drive Tate to school. Mom's taking over that chore. He claims his broken arm won't interfere with his driving, but Mom wouldn't hear of it."

"I'm sure that was an interesting conversation." Amusement laced Sawyer's words.

She rolled her eyes. "You don't want to know."

"That's a teenager." For a moment, they shared memories of dealing with Tate. "Our detour to the hospital has created a backlog. So I welcome your help."

"Good, because I'm here to work."

"Then let's get to it."

Over the next two weeks, the contractors started work at the rodeo grounds. In that time, Sawyer saw Erin watching him, but she never brought up the accident, how she'd rescued him and Tate. She didn't trade on what she did, but when he thought about what had happened, Erin's actions overwhelmed him. She'd risked her life to save Tate and him.

And with his mother's reappearance in his life, Erin said nothing about his attitude toward Sylvia, but, like a thorn in his side, his reaction to his mother sat between them. He wanted to talk to her about his mother, then he didn't want to talk. He didn't know what was wrong with him, except there was a tugging at his heart.

Finally, one Friday afternoon, after they'd inspected the concrete work done on the rodeo grounds by the company from Albuquerque, they started back to Sawyer's truck. He'd planned to talk to Erin about his mother, because the more they danced around the issue, the more the distance grew between them.

Mel zipped into the parking lot and stopped his truck next to Sawyer's. "I need to talk to you two," he said, slamming the truck door.

Sawyer stiffened, waiting for the complaint to be thrown out. He noticed Erin also braced herself.

Mel rubbed his neck, sighed and took a deep breath. Finally, he pulled a check out of his shirt pocket and handed it to Sawyer. When he unfolded the check, it was for more than the amount of the discrepancy Sawyer had discovered on the books for the concrete bill.

Sawyer glanced at Erin, then Mel. "What's this for?"

"I know you've been comparing final costs for the rodeo and talked to the folks at the concrete company, so I don't doubt you've found the discrepancy." He took a steadying breath and continued. "I ran into problems that year. My wife had health issues, and I took the money."

"That's more than the difference, Mel," Erin said.

He shrugged. "Interest."

"Why are you doing this?" Sawyer asked.

"Because I couldn't live with it anymore. I wanted a clean slate. Besides, you two have made a difference in Traci's life. Putting her in charge of the website for the rodeo has changed her. I see the little girl I loved after she's been lost for a long time." Mel turned to Erin. "You could've made it difficult for her. I know she wasn't nice to you and caused all sorts of problems, but you gave her a fair shot and it's made the difference. And, I know Traci was worried about Andy, but her worries proved to be unfounded."

He grinned. "I figure I might as well straighten out my life, too." Mel smiled. "It sure feels good."

Sawyer heard all sorts of lessons in Mel's words.

"If you feel a need to report me to authorities, I'm prepared to own up to my mistakes."

Sawyer had been quietly talking to the members about what he'd found. They'd debated it privately, not wanting to get the authorities involved, worried it would take away from the rodeo relaunch.

"It's not my call, Mel. I've discussed this with the board, but I think the repayment of the money might satisfy them. I don't know if they'll want you to resign your position," Sawyer said.

Mel's face didn't cloud up. "I understand, Sawyer. I'll work with the board however they want to do it." He looked around at the new concrete work done that morning. "Looks like the company did a first-rate job. I'm thinking the day this place reopens will be something to be proud of." He turned and walked back to his car, whistling.

Erin and Sawyer stood there staring.

"I've never seen Mel like that. It's an amazing thing." She smiled at him. "It seems God has a lot of things in store for us all, and we'll need to keep our hearts open to receive those blessings."

Sawyer flinched at her words. He watched her walk to his truck. The woman didn't play fair.

* * *

After dinner that Friday night, the hospital called, telling Mary that her husband had been okayed for release. During the call, the doctor talked to her about the aftercare and the therapy that her husband needed. Since there wasn't a facility in Tucumcari that could handle Detrick's needs, he'd either have to hire a therapist who would come to the house several times a week or rent a room in Albuquerque where they could stay and finish the rehab.

When Mary hung up, she explained the situation to Erin and Betty. Tate had been allowed to spend the night at the high school, helping with the senior play. His teacher would bring him home.

Betty spoke. "Stay with me and Nelson in Bluewater until Detrick finishes his therapy. We're only forty minutes away."

"That's a possibility." After several minutes discussing different plans, Betty left and went to her room.

"What do you think, Daughter?" Mary placed her napkin on the table.

"It would be easier on you and Dad to stay in Albuquerque. If you stayed with Auntie in Bluewater, I think the drive would be too much. But if you choose to do that, Tate will need somebody here. I'm willing to stay with him, but I think you should involve him in the decision." At least she thought that would be the approach Sawyer would suggest.

Sawyer. Erin would love to discuss this with him, but he wasn't talking. He'd removed himself emotionally from her, leaving her heart bleeding. She'd finally fallen in love with what she thought was the perfect man, but he'd seemed to disappear in an instant. She understood the scars on his heart but prayed God would give him the strength to see those scars and not let them have power over him anymore. When Erin looked up, she met her mother's knowing gaze.

"What's wrong?"

Erin didn't know how to put it into words. "Nothing."

"Then why are you frowning?"

"Things are going well with the rodeo. And all the support we get is encouraging." Erin told her mother what had happened with Mel that day.

"I know, I noticed a heaviness in Mel."

Her mother saw with her heart as much as with her eyes. "Daughter, I hear your words, and I see your heart. What is wrong?"

Was she ready to open up? Who better? "Sawyer."

"That's the name of the trouble. What has he done?"

"You knew that Sylvia was Sawyer's mother."

"No, I had not heard that."

Erin explained what had occurred. "Both Sawyer and his brother want nothing to do with her. There is no forgiveness in either of them. Caleb seems more set against his mother than Sawyer, but I think Sawyer received most of the beatings. It's as if I'm dealing with another man when the subject of his mom comes up.

"I haven't said anything to him about it, but it's there sitting between us much like a huge rock— cold and solid. He was the one who encouraged me to talk to both you and Dad and straighten things out, but he seems unwilling to follow his own advice."

"He's not the first man to say one thing and do another."

Truer words were never spoken. "I fear if he doesn't settle this with his mother, it will poison his life. I don't want that to happen to him."

Mary leaned back in her chair and beamed. "So your heart has succumbed."

She did a double take. "What?"

"Your heart beats for Sawyer." Mother had *that* smile on her face that made Erin crazy. When her mom had that particular look, it said she knew the truth even if the other person didn't.

"Of course I have a heart for him. He's hurting."

"Not that way. Your heart beats with his."

Erin opened her mouth to protest.

"I'm sorry, Daughter, but too often I've seen you walk away from a man who wanted to court you, and you'd have none of it. I've seen you freeze out a man who would try to get to know you. Now that your heart is on the line, you will need to learn patience, and grace."

Erin shook her head, wanting to dislodge the cotton in her ears. Surely she heard wrong. "What are you talking about?"

"Sawyer. He's touched your heart in a way no other man has."

Mary stood and placed a kiss on her daughter's forehead. "When the time is right, you'll understand. But don't fight it too long, or the opportunity will pass by."

"What are you talking about?" Erin still couldn't comprehend her mother's words. Or was it that she refused to understand?

"Trust your heart." With those final words, her mother left the room.

Erin stared at the doorway. She hated when her mom went all Native on her, giving her pieces of wisdom that she had to figure out. She wanted some concrete answers. And wanted them now.

Okay, Lord, I have no idea what Mom is talking about. Show me.

The next morning, after breakfast had been cleared, Mary called a family meeting. "I have decided to bring your father home. I will hire someone to come and give him therapy as often as he needs it. I know Betty misses her husband and needs to go home, today."

"But, Sister, I'm okay."

"Nelson misses you. It is time for you to go home. Besides, I don't want my son to be alone again, so his parents will be here." She turned to Tate. "I think if your father sees you, he'll know he has someone to work for. And he can be your support. I know he worries that you will drown in all this woman talk."

Erin hid her smile, not believing how her mother stated the problem. Mary wanted to get Tate involved with their father's recovery. "And he can see the progress on the rodeo grounds," Erin added.

"That would give him a goal," Betty said.

"What do you think, Son?" Mary asked.

Tate looked at Erin, then rubbed his hands over his jeans. "I think your plan, Mom, is a good one, but where are you going to find someone to come and help Dad with his therapy?"

"Before we leave the hospital today, I'll ask for a name."

"Sounds good," Tate replied.

"So, we're all agreed on the plan?" Mary asked. "Betty goes home and we go and get your father."

"Mom, why don't I stay here to get things ready? Besides, if you take Tate, he's stronger to help with Dad than me."

Tate's shoulders straightened, and he seemed to accept the responsibility. "I can do that."

"Then let's get going."

Erin went into town to see if Bob had any sort of shower chair for her father. He didn't but promised he'd order one.

Her next stop was at the rodeo office. The door stood locked. Where was Sawyer? She missed talking to him, discussing the rodeo; she missed being with him, missed his energy and the challenge he threw her way. There'd been a wall between them as they'd worked on the rodeo the past two weeks. He'd been polite, laughed with others, but she felt the barrier he'd thrown up, cutting himself off from her. She didn't know if others felt it, but seeing him every day and having him beyond her reach broke her heart.

Had his mother's reappearance thrown him that much off his stride that he couldn't recover? Was the hurt inflicted in his youth going to be the thing that defined his life? If that was the case, she needed to discover that now before more of her heart belonged to him.

Pausing by her truck door, she took a deep breath and finally admitted she loved him. Her knees buckled.

She didn't welcome the truth. If Sawyer couldn't find it in his heart to forgive his mother, how would he react to her if she made a mistake? Or a child of his own who made mistakes?

He had reasons for his feelings, the logical side of her brain argued, but her heart didn't buy it.

After a quick stop by Lulu's for a sandwich, she drove back home.

Not wanting to think about her confused feelings, she called Wind Dancer in from the field where all the horses were grazing. "Let's do barrels." That's all it took for her horse to come to her side. Erin quickly saddled Dancer, rode to the corral set up for barrel racing and started the workout. Maybe she could outrace any questions she had.

She lost track of time and used the workout to avoid facing the situation. She paused after the last run and realized Wind Dancer's sides heaved, but her horse would go again if asked. Erin knew it was time to stop. She patted the horse's neck. "Sorry, girl. I didn't mean to run you like that."

"It looked like you were running from something," Sawyer called out.

Her heart jumped at the sight of him. "I guess I'm not the only one."

He jerked as if she'd punched him in the chin. "I deserve that."

That wasn't the way to start a conversation with him.

Erin walked Wind Dancer around the corral, letting her cool down and catch her breath.

She didn't know what to say to him.

"Where is everyone?" He scanned the area.

"They went to Albuquerque to get Dad. The hospital called last night, telling us that Dad can be released. Aunt Betty went home."

"Why didn't you go with them?"

"The house needed to be readied for Dad, so I drove into town to get a couple of things, which will have to be ordered." She opened the corral gate and led the horse forward.

"I thought your mom and dad might stay close to the hospital for medical reasons."

"The family decided last night to bring him home and have a therapist come to the house. We thought Dad might recover quicker here. Also, Tate wouldn't be without his father again."

"Good idea."

She waited for him to say more, but he just stood there looking at her. "Why are you here? Did I forget to do something?" She guided Wind Dancer into the barn, stopped and grabbed the cinch under the horse and unbuckled it. When she started to pull the saddle off, Sawyer stepped in front of her and lifted it from the back of the horse. He put the saddle on the saddle stand outside the stalls.

"You didn't—"

He leaned forward and stopped her words with a kiss.

Erin didn't object. She wanted to throw her arms around the man, but Wind Dancer was at the end of the reins.

When he drew back, he rested his forehead against hers. "I've missed you."

Wind Dancer shook her head, setting the reins moving. Sawyer raised his head.

"I need to tend to her."

He gave her room and allowed Erin to unbuckle the horse's reins and turn her out in the corral.

Her heart pounded as she faced him. Her gaze caressed his face. The lines etched in his forehead and around his eyes spoke of his restless nights. Welcome to the club. She hadn't had a good night's sleep in several days, wondering about him, praying for him.

"I went by the office today, but found it locked," she told him.

"I'd gone out to talk to the artist hired to create the mural on the wall between the restrooms," Sawyer answered.

The artist proposed creating a mural of a scene involving several horses thundering across the desert. The drawing he submitted could be framed and used as a piece of art. She walked to the corral fence and watched Dancer.

He stood beside her. "It's peaceful out here. I can see why your grandfather settled in this place."

She knew instantly what he meant. She felt a special connection to the land and the ruggedness of this place. He'd understood, too.

"I've missed you," he said as he moved behind her and wrapped his arms around her waist.

His warmth and strength surrounded her, letting her know she could rest on him. "I've missed you, too, but you put up a wall I knew I couldn't scale."

His arms fell away, and he stepped back. "I just needed some time to sort things out. With Mom suddenly appearing in my life, there's lots of old baggage I'm tripping over."

She couldn't fault him for that. "And have you come to any decision? Know what to do with those old bags?"

"No. I talked with the pastor who helped Caleb and me when we were teens. You remember me talking about Pastor Garvey?"

"I do, and what did he say?"

Sawyer ran his hands through his hair, then over his face. "He said just forgive her. I didn't have to feel warm and fuzzy or have a blazing revelation, rather that it was a choice on my part." He shook his head. "I thought he was teasing us. He wasn't."

"And you find that hard to do?"

"It makes no sense. Surely there's more to it. It can't be that simple."

"What your pastor said isn't simple. It's the hardest thing you do, but you choose to do it."

"So says the only logical female I've ever run across."

"So says my pastor and yours."

He stepped closer. "And have you done that? Have you practiced what you preached?"

She heard the challenge in his question and the tone of his voice. "Yes. I had this smart cowboy tell me that my mother was unconsciously using me. I talked to her and worked things out. You should try it. I also talked to my dad, too. I forgave him for voting for you instead of me, because I believe Dad had a plan.

"It wasn't easy, nor did I feel like forgiving, but I did it."

Whirling, she marched into the barn. There were stalls that needed to be mucked out, and she couldn't think of a better time than now to deal with that mess.

Chapter Fifteen

Sawyer stood there watching Erin march into the barn with a full head of steam. She'd certainly turned his wisdom back on him. Nothing like getting smacked with one's own words.

He could stand out here and think, or he could help Erin with her chores. She might kick him out.

No, she wouldn't do that. No matter how mad or put out you were with someone, if they wanted to help muck out the stalls, you'd let them.

He grabbed a pitchfork and a broom and headed down the rows of stalls.

She didn't look up when he stepped into Duke's stall, which was next to the one she worked in, but she didn't object. That was a positive indication. They worked quietly for the next hour, cleaning and putting out fresh hay.

As he worked, he thought and prayed. Pastor Garvey and Erin had told him the same thing, and he trusted both of them. Pastor Garvey had taught him a lot of things, and never had he led him astray. He'd backed up his words with scriptures. It was easy to forgive someone if they'd just lied or cheated you out of some money, but what his mother did fell in a different league. But, he'd never read any qualifiers in the Bible. In other words, there were no limits on forgiveness.

They had just finished putting clean hay in the stalls when they heard engines. Vehicles pulled into the driveway.

Erin walked outside. He followed.

Two cars pulled into the parking area. The family sedan parked next to Erin's truck. Inside were Tate, Mary and her father. A second sedan parked beside his truck. Inside sat Sawyer's mother.

The kick to his gut wasn't as dramatic as it had been the first time she'd entered Detrick's room. This time he felt a peace.

Erin walked to her family's car and opened her dad's door, squatting in front of him. "Welcome home, Dad."

He grasped his daughter's hand. Silently he mouthed, *Home.*

Tate appeared by Erin's side. "Let me help, Dad."

Erin stood and stepped back. Tate grasped his father under the arm. Sawyer moved closer and took Detrick's other arm. Together all three of them walked into the house.

As Sawyer looked over his shoulder, he saw his mother embracing Erin.

Could he do it?

Over the weeks that he had shut Erin out, he knew he'd fallen in love. Could he fix the problem with his mother, and would it open up the way for him to tell Erin what was in his heart?

Mary opened the trunk, and Erin saw different pieces of equipment inside.

Sylvia stopped by Erin, reaching into the truck. "Let me help with unloading the equipment you'll need."

Erin hugged Sylvia. "I'm glad you're here. Are you going to be the one doing physical therapy with Dad?"

"No, I'm not going to do it, but your mom wanted me to come out here on my day off and show her how to set things up until the therapist gets here on Monday."

Erin wondered at her mom's plan. For the next hour, things were carried into the house and arranged to help Detrick and Mary deal with her father's hopefully temporary limitations.

After completing the setup, Mary invited Sylvia to stay the night. "It's too late for you to drive back," Mary argued. "I would feel better if you stayed."

"I hadn't planned on it. I have nothing with me."

"If you need anything, you can borrow it from me," Mary countered.

"Please stay," Erin added, understanding her mother's motives.

Sawyer hadn't left. Erin looked at him. His expression remained neutral.

"Thank you, I will," Sylvia replied.

"Good." Mary turned to Sawyer. "I'd like for you to share dinner with us, too. Both you and Sylvia have become very important to the Delong family, and we want to celebrate with you."

Sawyer remained quiet for a long time. Finally, he said, "Thank you, Mary, but I need to get back into town. I have some business to take care of."

Sylvia's disappointment showed in her face. No one said anything when Sawyer walked out of the house.

Erin started after him, but her mother caught her arm.

"Let him prove himself, Daughter. If his heart kicks in, then you know you can depend on him. If it doesn't, then you'll know to let him go."

Her mother's request made sense, but letting Sawyer walk away was the hardest thing Erin had ever done in her life.

Sawyer lay on his bed in his motel room and stared at the ceiling, wrestling with his decision to forgive. Was it worth it?

His entire future rested on *this* decision, because he knew if he chose to hold on to his resentment, he'd lose Erin.

Before he came to this city, there had been a calmness inside him, but now there was no peace. He knew both peace and love were within his grasp.

"Okay, Lord, You win. I forgive Mom."

He expected a huge weight would be lifted off his shoulders, but nothing happened. No lightning. No earthquake. He sat there a moment in the quiet. He'd done what he needed to do, so where was that marvelous moment of peace? It hadn't shown up. Now what?

He needed to tell his mom his decision. Glancing at the clock, he saw it was only ten fifteen. They would still be up, and he wanted to see his mother tonight.

With the radio off, the drive to the Delong ranch passed in silence, but the silence wrapped him in harmony.

He pulled by his mother's car and turned off the engine. Before he got to the back screen door, Erin appeared.

"Hi."

That soft welcome sound settled in his heart. He smiled at her, and she opened the door. Everyone at the table looked at him. "Excuse me for interrupting, but could I talk to Sylvia for a moment in private?"

Sylvia's eyes glistened.

"Why don't you go in the library?" Mary said. "Do you know where it is, Sawyer?"

He nodded and escorted his mother to the room. He looked straight into his mother's eyes and saw hope, fear and longing. "You asked me the other night if I could forgive you." He cleared his throat. "I've wrestled with the decision. How could I do it, let go of all the stuff in our past? But the pastor who taught both Caleb and me said it was a conscious action and not feeling.

"I forgive you, Mom, and want to put the past behind us and start over."

Tears ran down Sylvia's cheeks. "That's all I'm asking."

"You may not like me or who I've turned out to be, but I think we should get to know each other," Sawyer added. She started sobbing, and Sawyer didn't know what to do. He looked around and saw Mary and Erin standing at the door.

Mary motioned for him to hug his mother. He stepped forward and awkwardly wrapped his arms around Sylvia. She fell into his arms. He felt the sobs that racked her body and panicked. "Mom, did I do something wrong?"

She looked up and shook her head. "No. You did everything right."

That didn't make any sense. Why cry?

Erin slipped into the room and a placed a hand on his back. "You're doing good. Your mom is just overwhelmed with gratitude."

Sylvia stepped back and smiled at him. "You've given me a precious gift, Sawyer. Thank you."

Mary placed her arm around Sylvia's shoulders and walked her into the kitchen.

Erin stayed in the room with him. "That was a wonderful thing you just did for your mom."

He rubbed the back of his neck. "I've thought about what you said. Prayed. And I knew I had to toss that anger before I could tell you how I feel." He gently framed her face in his large hands. "Meeting you changed me. I saw a strong woman who could make a decision, argue her point of view and not give in to resentment or feel offended.

"You knocked me off my feet. No, you plowed me over, and I'm glad you did. I love you, Erin, and I want us to spend the rest of our lives together. Will you marry me?"

Tears ran down Erin's face, and this time he knew what to do. He kissed her and drew her to his chest.

When he pulled back, he wiped the tears from her cheeks.

"You're an amazing man. I never thought I'd ever meet someone like you. I'd be an idiot if I didn't say yes, and I'm no idiot."

"True," he whispered before kissing her again.

He heard laughter in the hall.

Epilogue

The opening day of the bicounty rodeo fell on a clear eighty-degree autumn day.

Sawyer walked up behind Erin and wrapped his arms around her waist. They'd been married two months. Their wedding was supposed to be a small affair at Lulu's, but everyone in the county came, so they'd moved it over to the convention center.

Erin looked around their still-unfinished house. They would operate their new business out of this place. The barns were the first thing done, and both Sawyer's and Erin's horses enjoyed their new home and each other.

The only thing that hadn't been resolved was that Caleb still hadn't come to grips with his mother. Sawyer assured her that his brother would.

When they arrived at the rodeo grounds, the first thing they saw was Caleb hugging his mother. His wife gave him a big kiss over the infant she held.

"It looks like your brother's come to terms with things," Erin whispered.

"I think it was that new baby girl that brought him around."

"So, you wouldn't mind having one of your own?"

He momentarily stared at her, and she got nervous. They hadn't planned to have kids so soon. Then understanding set in.

He hugged her and yelled, "Mom, you're going to be a grandma again in—" He turned to Erin.

"Seven and a half months, give or take."

"Around Valentine's Day." He let out a shout and laughed.

How amazing was what God had in store for her? She hadn't lost the bid for the redo of the rodeo; instead, she'd won. And won big.

* * * * *

Dear Reader,

I hope you've enjoyed the last of the original Rodeo Heroes series. Sawyer's story turned out to be the hardest one to write. He endured the most abuse of all three of my heroes—Caleb, Sawyer's brother, and Joel, his brother-in-law. When Sawyer met Erin Delong, a strong woman vying for the job of updating the bicounty rodeo, he expected her to go all weepy and pouty on him at her defeat. Instead, he found a determined woman ready to work with him. She challenged him at every turn but listened to his ideas. As they worked together Sawyer found his closely guarded heart opening up in ways he never thought possible. I had tears in my eyes when I finished writing this book. The story of the Good Samaritan found its way into the story, which I didn't plan, but it tied up everything nicely.

The lesson both Sawyer and Erin learned was God can take our disappointments and traumas and turn them around and make us stronger and whole.

I love to hear from readers. You can contact me through my website, www.leannharris.com.

Also check out my Facebook page, www.face book.com/authorLeannHarris.

Blessings,
Leann Harris

LARGER-PRINT BOOKS!

GET 2 FREE
LARGER-PRINT NOVELS
PLUS 2 FREE
MYSTERY GIFTS

Love Inspired®

SUSPENSE
RIVETING INSPIRATIONAL ROMANCE

Larger-print novels are now available...

YES! Please send me 2 FREE LARGER-PRINT Love Inspired® Suspense novels and my 2 FREE mystery gifts (gifts are worth about $10). After receiving them, if I don't wish to receive any more books, I can return the shipping statement marked "cancel." If I don't cancel, I will receive 4 brand-new novels every month and be billed just $5.49 per book in the U.S. or $5.99 per book in Canada. That's a savings of at least 19% off the cover price. It's quite a bargain! Shipping and handling is just 50¢ per book in the U.S. and 75¢ per book in Canada.* I understand that accepting the 2 free books and gifts places me under no obligation to buy anything. I can always return a shipment and cancel at any time. Even if I never buy another book, the two free books and gifts are mine to keep forever.

110/310 IDN GH6P

Name	(PLEASE PRINT)
Address	Apt. #
City	State/Prov.	Zip/Postal Code

Signature (if under 18, a parent or guardian must sign)

Mail to the **Reader Service**:
IN U.S.A.: P.O. Box 1867, Buffalo, NY 14240-1867
IN CANADA: P.O. Box 609, Fort Erie, Ontario L2A 5X3

**Are you a current subscriber to Love Inspired® Suspense books
and want to receive the larger-print edition?
Call 1-800-873-8635 or visit www.ReaderService.com.**

* Terms and prices subject to change without notice. Prices do not include applicable taxes. Sales tax applicable in N.Y. Canadian residents will be charged applicable taxes. Offer not valid in Quebec. This offer is limited to one order per household. Not valid for current subscribers to Love Inspired Suspense larger-print books. All orders subject to credit approval. Credit or debit balances in a customer's account(s) may be offset by any other outstanding balance owed by or to the customer. Please allow 4 to 6 weeks for delivery. Offer available while quantities last.

Your Privacy—The Reader Service is committed to protecting your privacy. Our Privacy Policy is available online at www.ReaderService.com or upon request from the Reader Service.

We make a portion of our mailing list available to reputable third parties that offer products we believe may interest you. If you prefer that we not exchange your name with third parties, or if you wish to clarify or modify your communication preferences, please visit us at www.ReaderService.com/consumerchoice or write to us at Reader Service Preference Service, P.O. Box 9062, Buffalo, NY 14240-9062. Include your complete name and address.

LISLP15

REQUEST YOUR FREE BOOKS!
2 FREE WHOLESOME ROMANCE NOVELS IN LARGER PRINT
PLUS 2
FREE
MYSTERY GIFTS

꘎꘎꘎꘎꘎꘎꘎꘎꘎꘎꘎꘎꘎꘎꘎꘎꘎꘎꘎꘎

HEARTWARMING™

꘎꘎꘎꘎꘎꘎꘎꘎꘎꘎꘎꘎꘎꘎꘎꘎꘎꘎꘎꘎

Wholesome, tender romances

YES! Please send me 2 FREE Harlequin® Heartwarming Larger-Print novels and my 2 FREE mystery gifts (gifts worth about $10). After receiving them, if I don't wish to receive any more books, I can return the shipping statement marked "cancel." If I don't cancel, I will receive 4 brand-new larger-print novels every month and be billed just $5.24 per book in the U.S. or $5.99 per book in Canada. That's a savings of at least 19% off the cover price. It's quite a bargain! Shipping and handling is just 50¢ per book in the U.S. and 75¢ per book in Canada.* I understand that accepting the 2 free books and gifts places me under no obligation to buy anything. I can always return a shipment and cancel at any time. Even if I never buy another book, the two free books and gifts are mine to keep forever.

161/361 IDN GHX2

Name _____ (PLEASE PRINT)

Address _____ Apt. #

City _____ State/Prov. _____ Zip/Postal Code

Signature (if under 18, a parent or guardian must sign)

Mail to the **Reader Service:**
IN U.S.A.: P.O. Box 1867, Buffalo, NY 14240-1867
IN CANADA: P.O. Box 609, Fort Erie, Ontario L2A 5X3

* Terms and prices subject to change without notice. Prices do not include applicable taxes. Sales tax applicable in N.Y. Canadian residents will be charged applicable taxes. Offer not valid in Quebec. This offer is limited to one order per household. Not valid for current subscribers to Harlequin Heartwarming larger-print books. All orders subject to credit approval. Credit or debit balances in a customer's account(s) may be offset by any other outstanding balance owed by or to the customer. Please allow 4 to 6 weeks for delivery. Offer available while quantities last.

Your Privacy—The Reader Service is committed to protecting your privacy. Our Privacy Policy is available online at www.ReaderService.com or upon request from the Reader Service.

We make a portion of our mailing list available to reputable third parties that offer products we believe may interest you. If you prefer that we not exchange your name with third parties, or if you wish to clarify or modify your communication preferences, please visit us at www.ReaderService.com/consumerchoice or write to us at Reader Service Preference Service, P.O. Box 9062, Buffalo, NY 14240-9062. Include your complete name and address.

HW15

READERSERVICE.COM

Manage your account online!

- Review your order history
- Manage your payments
- Update your address

> *We've designed the*
> *Reader Service website*
> *just for you.*

Enjoy all the features!

- Discover new series available to you, and read excerpts from any series.
- Respond to mailings and special monthly offers.
- Connect with favorite authors at the blog.
- Browse the Bonus Bucks catalog and online-only exculsives.
- Share your feedback.

Visit us at:
ReaderService.com